CHASING TEMPTATION

Original Sinners One

Micah Hayden

ISBN 9780473553470 (paperback)
ISBN 9780473553487 (Kindle)

Cover design by: Micah Hayden

CHAPTER ONE

T he shop was like any other small-town antique store. There was no breathing room between the aisles, and the high shelves were crowded precariously with dilapidated knick knacks. A musty smell permeated the air. I didn't expect to find much here. Maybe some old jewelry or furniture to refurbish.

The man at the counter was as much of an antique as anything he sold. His face was lined with deep creases, and what little hair he had left clung to the sides of his paper-skinned scalp. He squinted through thick glasses at an old paperback, licking his fingers every time he needed to turn a page. He was so engrossed that I had no doubt I could have lifted anything off the shelves and slipped it into my pocket without being noticed. But that wasn't my style. Rhett Beach was no petty thief. Not anymore. Now, I was a professional.

I wiped a layer of grime off a glass cabinet and peered inside. A stone-blue clay jar caught my attention instantly, half-hidden behind a floral tea set. I wasn't sure if it was my education or intuition that drew my attention to the dusty jar, but once I saw it, I knew without a doubt it needed to be mine.

"Can I look inside this cabinet?" I asked the man behind the counter.

He nodded, not looking up from his book.

The glass cabinet didn't look like it had been opened in years. I slid it open, and my fingertips were immediately powdered with dust. I gently shifted the teapot aside so I could see the jar properly. Shivers coursed through my body.

The sides of the vessel were engraved. Like a lot of ancient friezes, the illustrations were explicit. They told an ancient story of sex and murder. I'd never seen anything like it before.
I was able to accurately date any artifact back to at least 300BC, but this pyxis belonged to deeper, older eras. I needed to have it.

"Is it okay if I pick this up?" I called.

The old man mumbled something that sounded close enough to 'yes.' I brushed my fingers over the jar, half-expecting the old clay to crumble. It was surprisingly sturdy. Nonetheless, I picked it up as though I was handling a fragile newborn baby. Despite the layer of grime, the jar shimmered in the light. This was the find of a lifetime.

The pyxis was handmade. The base was uneven, and the walls sloped asymmetrically. It was probably my imagination, but I could have sworn the jar was as warm as if it had just left the kiln. It fit in the palm of my hand, heavier than its size betrayed. Something must have been inside, perhaps something even more precious than the pyxis itself. I made to twist off the lid. It wouldn't give.

"That jar doesn't open," croaked a frail voice.

I started. I had been so transfixed by the pyxis that I had forgotten I wasn't alone in the room.

Cupping my precious discovery between my palms, I sauntered to the counter. The old man had put his book down while I was staring at the pyxis, and now he was peering at me over the rim of his glasses. I tried not to look too excited.

"How much for this jar?"

If the old man who ran this store knew how much the pyxis was worth, there would be no chance I'd afford it.

"It's old, that one," he said. He skimmed his tongue over parchment-dry lips.

"How much do you want for it?" I asked.

He pursed his wrinkled lips. "Two hundred dollars."

I tried not to look too taken back. Even if the vessel was a fake—and I was almost positive it wasn't—it would have been worth more than that.

"I can do two hundred." It took every ounce of self-control not to let my excitement show on my face.

I handed the money over—I always paid in cash, an old habit from my drug-dealing days—and the elderly man wrapped the clay jar in newspaper. His hands shook so much, I might have aged a year before he was done.

At last, I zipped the pyxis into the leather sling bag strapped across my chest. I was glad to be getting out of here.

The second I stepped outside, sweat prickled up through my pores. The air was humid and sticky. I tugged my T-shirt away from my body. Despite the heat, the clouds were low and grey, rendering me claustrophobic.

A butchery and a gas station flanked the antiques store, the only buildings for miles. Farmland stretched out as far as I could see. I couldn't hear a single car, just the faint bleating of sheep in the distance.

I usually liked tiny rural communities. I never ran into anyone from my past in these places, and I didn't stick around long enough to connect with anybody new—not for longer than one night, anyway. My nomadic lifestyle rejected commitment. Sometimes it got lonely, but it was better to be lonely than to devote myself to someone who'd abandon me.

Today, I wished there were more people around. The hairs on the back of my neck stood on end. I was paranoid from the knowledge that a priceless artifact was tucked in my bag, sandwiched between my wallet and a bottle of lube. The back of my neck crawled as though someone was breathing over my shoulder. When I turned around, there was no-one there.

From this cluster of shops, it was a thirty-minute

walk to get back to the campground where my van was parked. Half an hour had never seemed so long. I walked as fast as the heat would allow. The weight of the little blue jar prodded unmistakably into my chest. I jerked my head around every few seconds to make sure no-one was following me and saw nothing but worn road and long, yellow grass.

The closer I got to the campground, the more intense my feeling of being watched became. I became sure it was instinct, not imagination. My shoulders tensed, ready to throw a punch, and the muscles in my thighs coiled tightly in anticipation of sprinting away. I glanced over my shoulder again.

Something was stalking me through the stiff grass. It looked like a dog, but it was bigger than any dog I'd ever seen. Its tawny fur was matted, and the muscles in its haunches rippled with every motion of its lanky limbs. I had been prepared to run, but now I was sealed to the spot in terror. The animal growled, and the sound cut through the air like a jagged knife.

My mouth was suddenly desert-dry. The dog's eyes fixed on me and glinted red in the dying sunlight. The resolve in them was almost human. *This animal was coming for the kill.*

CHAPTER TWO

I turned my back on the dog and stared desperately down the road. I willed a car to appear and rescue me from the predator, but none appeared.

Slick sweat dripped down my back, no longer simply from the heat. Fear froze the blood in my veins. I was sure the animal could smell my terror and hear my suddenly racing heart. I marched forward as though if I didn't look at it, it might disappear.

My skin crawled. The sky was swelling with the promise of rain, getting darker every second. Orange beams streamed through ever-smaller cracks in the clouds. I was only five minutes away from the campground. It felt like an eternity.

I heard another growl from behind me, even closer this time. Despite my better instincts, I turned around. I fully expected to see a flash of canine teeth flying at my throat. Instead, I found myself face-to-face with the most beautiful woman I'd ever seen. Nearly-black eyes contrasted violently with her milky skin. Her hair was long and chestnut-brown, and it cascaded down her back like a veil. A shiny black dress clung to curves that would have put a Victoria's Secret model to shame. If I hadn't been gay, I would have been speechless.

As it was, I was terrified. She smiled, and I was paralyzed with fear. I had never seen anyone so menacing before. I stumbled, desperate to run away, terrified to turn my back on her.

"Who are you?" I asked weakly. "Where did you come from?"

She smiled and cocked her head too far to the left. It was an unnatural posture, and it made my stomach churn.

"Hello," she said sweetly.

I stepped back, dizzy. She bared her teeth into a grimace that might have been a smile on anyone else.

"Who the hell are you?" I repeated.

"That doesn't matter."

Quicker than a bolt of lightning, the woman struck me. Sharp nails slashed across my face, and I fell back. I cradled my arms around my chest so I wouldn't break the clay jar in my bag. My face stung and throbbed. The woman crouched over me.

I'd never been in a situation like this before. Apparently, my instinct was neither fight nor flight. I froze instead. It was a weak, pathetic response. I would have judged myself for it if I could have thought anything other than '*I don't want to die.*'

I touched my face, and my hand came back red with my own blood.

"Why are you doing this?" I pleaded. "What do you want from me?"

She laughed, a surprisingly gentle, bell-like sound, and then her hand was around my throat. She squeezed. I twisted my head to try and get out of her grip. She had me like a vice.

"You have something I want."

The pyxis. I instinctively clutched my bag closer. I wasn't going to give up my new prized possession that easily. I wanted to at least try and fight. Even if my stubborn body refused to move. Even if I was suddenly unable to do anything except stare at this terrifying woman.

If she were a regular mugger, I would have thrown my wallet toward her and run away. There was no reason to value this jar over my life, but I was struck with a cold feeling in the pit of my belly every time I thought of giving it away. I knew, on some primal level, that it was supposed to be mine.

"The jar, please, " my attacker cooed.

She tilted her head to the side and batted her eyelashes. Her hand left my throat, and her fingers danced over my lips. I got the impression that she was trying to seduce me, but she wasn't my type.

"I- I don't have a jar," I said. I finally managed to scramble out of her grip and to my feet. My legs tensed in preparation to run.

"I don't appreciate liars," the woman said. Her voice was suddenly cold, and her smile vanished.

"Give it to me!"

She stepped toward me. I tried to run. She caught me by the wrist and pulled me close, so close that her lips were right next to mine. Her face twisted into an inhuman expression, and her dazzling beauty was gone in an instant. I struggled to inhale.

The woman leaned even closer, and I thought for a crazy moment that she was going to kiss me. But then she spun away. My hand was torn from her grip. Before I knew what was going on, she tumbled to the ground at my feet.

A man had joined the fight. He towered over the woman, his lips twisted in a snarl. Adrenaline must have rendered me delirious, because I could have sworn I recognized that profile, his sharply pointed nose and strong jaw. The man looked from the woman to me, and the fierce, familiar expression on his face assured me I wasn't making things up. It was really him.

Dorian Taylor.

Dorian had aged in the last ten years, but the man looming over me was unmistakably the same boy I'd grown up with. He was the first guy I'd fallen in love with. I'd given everything to Dorian, and then he up and left my life when we were seventeen without so much as a goodbye.

I had no idea how he approached us so stealthily, but no matter how it happened, *Dorian was here.* Protecting me.

Dorian had always been handsome. Now, he was an honest-to-god Adonis. His cheekbones were sharp in his chiseled face, and his lips were soft, red, and plump. The ends of his wavy brown hair just brushed his shoulders. A day or two's worth of stubble shaded his jaw. Tight jeans and a black T-shirt hugged his body like a second skin, and golden rings circled the fingers on his right hand like a classy knuckle duster. I was struck dumb by the sight of him. I had never expected to see Dorian again, and certainly not in a situation like this.

His brow furrowed over wild, amber eyes. It was a painfully familiar expression of shock and awe. It was the expression he'd worn when he first saw me naked, years ago. He held my gaze for a beat too long before he glanced back at the woman on the ground between us.

"You should leave, Mara."

She hissed at him. "I'm not going anywhere."

"I'd rather not kill you," said Dorian smoothly. "But you know I will if I have to."

Mara picked herself up off the ground, and before I knew what was going on, she and Dorian had each other in a stranglehold. Dorian made eye contact with me over Mara's head.

"Run," he mouthed.

My legs were numb, and I was frozen in fear. I didn't want to leave him. If I did what Dorian said, I might never see him again. But when he ordered me to run, I was compelled to obey. I turned on my heels and sprinted away from my mysterious attacker and my even more enigmatic savior.

My pulse throbbed in my ears. Dorian yelled behind me, and I was tempted to look back, but I didn't dare. The air began to strangle my lungs, and the muscles in my legs burned. I kept running. I didn't stop until I reached the campground.

There was a vacationing family milling around near the picnic tables. I stilled and took some deep breaths to compose myself and look less like I'd just been running for my life.

I refused to think about what had happened yet. If it were possible, I would have tried to forget about the whole thing. But Mara's face would doubtless haunt my nightmares. Besides, I'd spent ten years trying to forget about Dorian. There was no reason to think I'd finally succeed now.

I flashed a smile at the family, who gave me an odd look in return. I must have been a mess, soaked in sweat and with bloody slashes across my face. I hoped they wouldn't call the authorities. I had no capacity to deal with cops tonight.

Before I got my van, I slept in my car and paid steep rent on a crappy apartment I was never home long enough to use. After one particularly cold night on the side of the road with a drained battery, I impulsively bought a small motorhome second-hand from a rental company who were upgrading their fleet. Best decision I ever made.

Back then, recreational drugs and casual sex were my religion. At my request, my man-of-the-moment coated the van with psychedelic whirls and cells of enamel paint. The colors and patterns that had seemed cool to my high-as-balls twenty-one-year-old self now looked gaudy and conspicuous. Over the last year, the paint had finally started to fade and scrape away, leaving gashes of naked metal behind.

My van was parked at the far end of the campground, where the mud floor met a wall of green trees. This site was secluded from the rest of the camp. I usually liked isolation, but right now, I wished I had company.

I unlocked the door and stepped inside. The van embraced me with its familiarity, and I immediately felt safer. The ceiling was low enough to scrape my hair, and I was too graceless to weave around the cramped furniture without knocking into the edges. But for all its faults, this was *home*. Even the perfume of stale incense soothed me.

This van was only big enough for one person, which made it easy to keep to myself. Nothing compared to the freedom of being able to pack up my van whenever I pleased, with no-one to tell me where to go or what to do.

Inside, the van was like any other old motorhome, except for the cubby I had built next to the coffee-stained stovetop. The pale wooden cubicle was one-of-a-kind. Locked drawers and secure cabinets were built into three tall, wood-paneled walls crowded around a slender desk. This was where I studied my most precious finds and worked out what they were worth.

I sat in the hard chair by my desk and grazed my hand down a wall until I found a groove in the wood.

I pushed my fingertips down hard, and a discreet switch gave way under my touch. The door to a secret cabinet swung open. Inside was a small, grey safe.

I slipped my leather bag away from my chest and gently took out the pyxis. I was half-afraid it might have broken when I fell—when Mara pushed me to the ground—but it was still in the same condition as in the antique store.

It was such a simple object to have already caused me so much trouble. I must have found something precious. I turned it over in my hands, running my fingers over the rough, oddly warm clay. It was rare, almost unheard of, to find something this old in a thrift store. It was certainly unprecedented to find something from this era of Greek history with such detailed engravings. I skimmed my fingers over the etchings, and my breath trembled. I tried to wedge the lid off again, but there was no budging it.

I wanted to look at the jar in closer detail and decode what the frieze on the sides might have meant, but exhaustion had my hands shaking and my mind fried. I found myself jumping at the slightest sound outside the motorhome, no matter how deeply I tried to breathe.

I touched the fingerprint scanner on the outside of my safe. It beeped, and the door swung open. Some people might have thought I was paranoid about my security, but I considered myself cautious instead.

The safe was lined with bubble wrap in case I had

to skid the van to an abrupt stop. I rewrapped the clay jar in newspaper for extra protection and shut it away. Once the safe was locked and the wall was closed, there was no way for anyone to know where the artifact was hidden.

Now I had nothing to distract me from the terror starting to settle in my bones. I half wondered if I had hallucinated what had happened to me this afternoon, but then I touched my face. My fingers connected with the fresh ridges of a new scar.

A glance in the mirror showed me a reflection I hardly recognized. Four symmetrical lines of red stood out on my face where Mara had struck me with her nails. *That was going to leave a mark.* The scars might have improved another man's street cred, but on me, they looked like a loser's wounds.

I was on the skinny side of lean, and if I were a couple of inches taller, I might have been described as lanky rather than scrawny. At least my beard gave the impression I was older than twenty-seven. Sometimes, when I wasn't bleeding from the face, I even looked distinguished. I wasn't drop-dead-gorgeous like Dorian, but I was decent looking, and I didn't have trouble finding guys to satisfy my sexual appetite.

Hookups replaced real connections for me a long time ago, and that was the way I liked it. My relationship with Dorian had been my first and last real romance, and I balked at the idea of letting someone in again. It was better to have a hard heart than a broken one.

There was too much going on in my mind. My head was on the brink of exploding from confusion. The longer I stared at my reflection, the less I could deny what I had experienced. It had all happened so fast, my memories blurred together. The reddish glint in that feral dog's eyes, Mara's terrifyingly beautiful expression, and then... *Dorian*.

Dorian had grown up to be even more gorgeous than I anticipated. The planes of his rugged face intoxicated me, and his muscles made my heart pound for reasons unrelated to adrenaline.

I grabbed a threadbare top and a pair of pajama pants out of my basket of clean clothes and tossed them onto the futon sofa to wear once I undressed.

I pulled off my sweat-stiff shirt, and someone knocked on my door. I froze. My naked chest heaved. I was an introvert at the best of times, and tonight, the last thing I wanted was a random knock on my door. I didn't want to see another face until I'd slept for at least eight hours.

"I know you're in there," said a calm male voice. *Dorian's voice.* Had he followed me here?

I remained silent. Anything I said would have sounded pathetic, and my mouth was too dry to form words. Dorian had no need to follow up after saving my life, but he was checking that I was okay anyway. I tried not to let my heart flutter, and my gut flipped defiantly.

Dorian jiggled the door handle. "Let me in, Rhett."

The sound of my name on Dorian's lips yanked at

my heartstrings like I was in high school again. His voice was higher than you might expect from looking at him, but every word carried a resonant rumble. It had been almost ten years since I last saw Dorian, and even after all this time, he made my blood burn hotter than any other man.

I peeked through the window. Dorian's expression was concerned and stern at once.

"Don't you want to know why Mara came after you?" asked Dorian.

I was desperate for answers, but I knew that if I let Dorian in, I wouldn't be able to stop old feelings resurfacing. I swallowed and reminded myself that I had willpower now. Emotions didn't have the same hold on me as they used to. Sure, I was attracted to Dorian and sure, I was desperate to know what kind of man the last ten years had turned him into. But that didn't mean I had to fall for him again.

"Come on, Rhett. Let me in, and I'll tell you everything."

He always knew what buttons to push. "Everything?"

"Everything."

CHAPTER
THREE

Dorian stepped into my van and closed the door behind him. I instantly regretted inviting him inside. Even on those rare occasions I entertained visitors, I had never felt so cramped and crowded here before. Dorian ran his eyes up and down my body, and I became acutely aware that I was naked from the waist up.

Now that we weren't in a life-or-death situation, I could look at my ex-boyfriend properly. It was like a god had gone out of their way to craft the perfect specimen of manliness, and they'd come up with Dorian. His dark hair was tousled, and a crooked smirk sat on his plush lips. Dorian always had been poised, and as an adult, he had even more command over every muscle. He stood statue-still, while I shook like a damn vibrator.

A leather vest was slung over Dorian's tight T-shirt, and a bruise rested like a grimy halo around one of his eyes. He must have got himself injured protecting me. That knowledge made my heart pump faster.

So Dorian didn't want me to get murdered. So what? That didn't mean he wanted me.

"What's going on, Dorian?" I asked weakly. "How did you find me? What happened to you? Where have you been?"

"You're as curious as ever," said Dorian. His somber expression lightened. "It's good to see you again, Rhett."

I wanted to return the compliment, but I didn't know how I felt about reuniting with Dorian. I thought I'd trained myself out of succumbing to emotions like love and betrayal, but now that I was face-to-face with Dorian, it was clear I'd failed. My face was hot, and my pulse was racing. Ten years on, the heartbreak was still fresh. I took a deep breath, reminding myself how good it felt to have no attachments. There was no reason things should change. After I got my answers, he could leave. No, *I* could leave.

"You said you'd tell me why Mara came after me," I said stiffly. "I assume it's got something to do with the pyxis."

Dorian nodded. "Mara has been searching for that jar for years. She'd do anything to get her hands on it."

"Why?"

"It's valuable."

If the pyxis was worth so much that Mara was willing to kill me over it, it was worth enough to change my life. With that kind of cash, there'd be no more cold showers at crappy campgrounds, no more eating ramen for weeks on end, and no more driving on bald tires because I couldn't afford a mechanic. This little jar could have been my lucky break. Only most strokes of good fortune weren't accompanied by attacks from ferocious super-model-esque women—or rescues from enigmatic ex-boyfriends. There must have been more to this than money.

Dorian stepped closer to me, encroaching on my space. His body heat washed over me, and I was struck with lust so powerful it rooted me to the spot. My mind threatened to go blank. I cut a glance down to his groin. His cock was bigger than I remembered, the outline cupped by tight denim pants. My own dick lifted in response to the sight of his bulge. If I let myself give into my instincts, I would have fallen to my knees and offered to serve my ex then and there.

Focus, Rhett. Now wasn't the time to get horny. I had to keep my mind on the topic at hand.

I forced myself to look back at Dorian's face, and I cringed at his broad smirk. He knew exactly what I'd been staring at.

"Who is Mara?" I asked.

"It's better if you don't know." Dorian touched my cheek. The scratches on my face burned, and my heart leapt. "She hurt you quite badly, didn't she?"

"It looks worse than it is," I said. I pulled away from Dorian before he charmed me any further. "I don't want your sympathy. I want answers. Who the fuck is Mara? Why did she want the pyxis, really? I know it's not all about money. I'm not stupid."

"You always were too clever for your own good." Dorian completely ignored my questions. "Have you been able to get the jar open?"

"No." I set my jaw. Dorian's promise to tell me everything was seeming more hollow with every half-answer he gave.

"Good." Dorian sighed and rubbed his temples with his forefingers. "That's good, at least."

"Why is that good?"

Dorian didn't respond.

"I let you inside so that you'd explain what the hell is going on. So explain."

"What the hell, indeed." Dorian's lips twitched into a smile like he was laughing at his own private joke.

I had no idea what was supposed to be so funny, and I'd had enough of his cryptic bullshit. "Tell me what's inside the fucking jar, Dorian."

"That's none of your concern."

I took a deep breath to steady my nerves. My emotions were running high, and I didn't want to do or say anything I'd regret.

"What does any of this have to do with you, any- way? What sort of weird shit did you get into after you left me?" My words tasted bitter. Ten years on, I was still hung up on the way Dorian had bailed on me, and I was doing a piss poor job of hiding it.

"I didn't want to leave you."

"Then why-" I shook my head. I wasn't going to go there. I wasn't going to let any hope brew in my heart when all Dorian wanted was the pyxis. This wasn't about me. "Forget it."

Dorian looked me in the eyes for a beat too long and wordlessly stripped off his leather vest.

"What are you doing?" My mouth was dry.

"I'm getting more comfortable."

Dorian's tight T-shirt clung to his broad shoulders and skimmed over powerful muscles toward a narrow waist. I knew he was undressing to distract me, but damn it, it was working. How could I not be entranced by that body?

Dorian had always been more athletic than me, but he'd become even stronger since I last saw him. No man had the right to be that ripped. If he chose to pin me down, I would be entirely at his mercy. And god, that was exactly where I wanted to be.

I exercised enough to stay in shape. Gas was expensive, and I liked to keep my muscles moving, so I walked more than I drove. My pecs and abs were defined under a thin layer of fat, and my legs were long and lean. I usually thought I looked decent, but compared to Dorian, my average looks were even more ordinary.

I tried to keep my arousal at bay, but I was getting more turned on with every breath I took. If I kept sharing my personal space with Dorian, I wouldn't be able to keep from throwing myself at him. I stumbled backward until my knees hit the seat of my futon and hurriedly sat down to hide my boner.

Without invitation, Dorian sat next to me. There wasn't enough room on the futon to maintain a respectable distance. His aura radiated heat against me, making me sweat.

"I need to get that jar off you, Rhett. It's important."

There it was. The real reason he followed me home. He didn't want me. I should have known that, but it still stung.

"I paid for it," I said. "It's mine."

Dorian leaned in, a breath away from me now. I was trapped like a rat in a cage, but I didn't want to escape.

"I can reimburse you," he said. "I'll give you back whatever you paid."

"No, thanks." I forced my spine straight in a show of fake confidence. "It was a huge bargain."

"Tell me what it's worth. I'll pay that."

"You can't afford it."

"I can. Trust me."

Trust him? Not a chance.

Ten years ago, Dorian lived on charity. His mom worked three jobs, and they still barely got by. Everyone in our small town knew the two of them struggled to afford food. My parents hadn't been well off either, but they fed Dorian dinner every night. Until they found out he was more than my best friend, anyway. After that, Dorian was on his own again, and our relationship was relegated to secrecy unless I wanted to be cast aside too.

I always wondered if my parents' homophobia was one of the reasons Dorian left town. But maybe leaving had been the right decision, if he was now in a position to pay me what the pyxis was worth.

What the hell had happened to Dorian to turn him into someone like this? All confidence, sex appeal, and wealth. He'd always been cocky and hot, but this was different.

"The pyxis needs to be examined by an expert. I'll only sell it to a museum."

"What if I told you I worked for a museum?"

"I'd call you a liar, and I'd tell you I'm not settling for less than the truth."

Dorian's expression was suddenly threatening. "As long as you have that jar, you're in danger. Don't you understand that?"

"I'm starting to." I gulped. My heart hadn't raced this urgently in a long time. "But I'm not going to change my mind. You can't scare me, Dorian."

"Don't be so naive." Dorian's composure facade slipped away. "For all you know, you should be scared of me. I might want to hurt you."

"Do you want to hurt me?" I asked outright, forcing my voice not to tremble.

A muscle in Dorian's jaw twitched, and his eyes hardened. For a second, I thought he might say yes. But he sighed. "I prefer to deal in pleasure than pain."

"Oh."

A hint of amusement teased stern lines away

from the corners of Dorian's lips, and his smile sent my heart somersaulting.

No matter what existed between us years ago, Dorian and I had different goals now. He wanted the pyxis for himself. I planned to sell it to a museum. If he had been anyone else, I would have sent him away by now.

But he was *Dorian*.

My aching cock pushed against my zipper, and it took all of my self-control not to whip it out already.

The last time anyone sucked my dick, it had been through a hole in the wall at a dingy truck stop. I had nothing against cruising. I was on the road so much that those kinds of hookups were a crucial relief. But it felt like forever since another man's naked limbs were entwined with mine. Now that Dorian was in front of me, all I wanted was to be with him, to have nothing between us, and to see how much we'd both improved in bed since we were young lovers.

"What kind of pleasure do you deal in?" I asked weakly.

"Don't you remember?" His voice was almost a purr. He leaned in closer to me.

My willpower broke. I snaked my arms around Dorian's neck and pulled him into a kiss. He responded eagerly. Dorian had always been a good kisser, but now he used his lips so expertly it was almost unbearable. He drew me close so that I was half-lying on top of him on the sofa. My erection poked into his inner groin. I noticed with a swell of excitement that his cock was as hard as my own.

I needed to touch it.

I didn't want to think about how reckless I was being. I didn't trust Dorian, but that didn't mean I couldn't want him. His body was hard and responsive under me, and his hands caressed every part of my skin he could reach. I craved more.

While we kissed, fire rippled through my muscles and throbbed steadily toward my balls. I slipped my hands under Dorian's shirt. His hot skin quivered as I trailed my fingertips above his waistband, teasing the flat expanse of skin above his groin. The more I touched him, the more I needed to touch him. I ripped his shirt off over the top of his head.

Dorian's body seemed sculpted by a classical artist. His skin was smooth and pale, and bars of metal pierced his pink nipples. He had always been stunning, but now, he was like the spawn of a god and a supermodel. My heart skipped a beat, and I nearly came in my pants just looking at him. I ran my fingers up and down the ridges of his abs, and he made a responsive gasp.

God, yes. I loved that gasp. The more I touched Dorian, the more I wanted him. I fumbled for his belt and hastily unbuckled it.

Dorian grabbed me by my chin and made me look at him. He wasn't rough with me, but I couldn't escape him if I tried. I memorized every detail of his face, studying the light creases in his skin and the rough stubble on his chin. He had changed a lot since I saw him last, and he was somehow even more attractive now.

"Are you sure you want to do this?" he asked.

"Yes," I said earnestly. The least I deserved was a good pounding, after all he'd put me through.

"Good." His words caught on his breath, but no matter how ragged he sounded, his voice enchanted me.

I undid the fly on his jeans button-by-button. It took too long. I needed to see Dorian's cock already. I slipped off the sofa so that I was kneeling on the ground before him. Deja vu flooded me. This was an intimately familiar position for the two of us, and it was like nothing I'd ever experienced before.

Once Dorian's pants were down, I got an eyeful of the erection pitching a tent in silky, violet boxers. There was a damp spot of precum where the head of his cock met the fabric. I mouthed it through the fabric, and Dorian let out a moan that made every cell in my body sing. I teased his waistband with my fingers again, trying to get him as desperate for my mouth as I was to taste him.

Dorian let out a frustrated grunt. He yanked his underwear down and kicked it across the floor, along with his pants. His cock lurched out immediately, and I was faced with the most perfect dick I'd ever seen.

I loved cock. Fat cocks, skinny cocks, long cocks, short cocks... I eagerly pleased them all. I was like the Dr. Seuss of dick: I would take cock here or there, I'd give my ass up anywhere.

But Dorian's was the best cock I'd ever seen. His uncut dick was huge, easily as thick as a beer can and twice as long. Thick veins snaked around the sides of his package, and heavy, hairy balls hung pendulously by the base. His shaft was the same golden tan of his body, and I wondered if he suntanned naked. The thought of him nude on a bright, sandy beach made me throb even more urgently.

"Are you just going to stare?" asked Dorian hoarsely.

Oh no, I was going to do a lot more than stare. A cock this perfect deserved my full attention. I opened my mouth and wet my lips, working out where to start. I wrapped my hand around the base of Dorian's dick and slowly stroked upward. His cock burned even hotter than the rest of his body. I touched it, and it flexed responsively.

I filled my mouth with saliva and touched the tip of my wet tongue to Dorian's cockhead. He let out a groan that shivered through me. Encouraged, I opened my mouth wider and made out with the tip of his dick. I lavished it in sloppy kisses. He thrust his hips up, but I wasn't going to swallow him down yet. I brushed my tongue against the seam of skin just under his cockhead, where it connected to his shaft, and taunted him with light licks rather than sucking him in earnest. My tongue followed the veins on his cock like a map, twitching with extra pressure over the spots I knew he was most sensitive.

Dorian gripped my hair and whimpered. I pulled

away, looked up at him, and wiped spit off the bottom of my chin.

"You remember how I like it," he breathed.

"I do," I said.

Everything about Dorian was impossible to forget.

"Suck me harder," he said.

It was a command, not a request, and I had to obey. I took Dorian's cock in my mouth, and my jaw strained to fit around it. I covered my teeth with my lips so that I wouldn't accidentally graze his shaft. Dorian's cock curved in such a way that it was easy to suck deep, despite the size. I sucked him down and slowly pulled back until his shaft was exposed again, glossy with my saliva.

"You're a tease," growled Dorian.

"You know it."

"I need more," he grunted. "Suck me deep, Rhett. Show me how good you are with that pretty mouth."

I acquiesced and engulfed Dorian's cock in my mouth again. This time, he didn't give me the chance to pull away, even if I had wanted to. He seized me by the back of my head and forced me further down his cock until it slotted into my throat. My gag reflex threatened to lurch, but I repressed it. I swallowed Dorian's cock deeper until my face was buried in his sweet, musky pubes.

Dorian's balls were wet with my spit. I gently rolled them between my fingers. He let out a howl and began facefucking me in earnest, pummelling my mouth with his big cock. My eyes streamed. I looked up at the man who owned me. His face was contorted in bliss. He pumped my mouth harder, and I took it gladly.

I finally gave in to my own dick's aching pleas and unzipped my fly. I was leaking so much precum that I didn't even need to spit for lubrication. I rubbed my shaft up and down, relieved for the friction at last.

Dorian released me, and I gasped for breath. I expected him to shove his cock back into my throat as soon as I had replenished the oxygen in my lungs. Instead, he leaned back and looked at me. I was sure I was a mess, kneeling on the ground, my pants halfway down my thighs, and my hand furiously working my cock.

"Get up," said Dorian.

Every muscle in my body trembled. I clambered to my feet. Dorian stayed seated, his head at waist-height. He smiled up at me, and I melted. Nothing had changed in ten years. I was still as smitten with this man as I'd ever been.

Dorian grabbed me by the waist and pulled me close. I tumbled forward, and then I was sitting on his lap. Our dicks pressed up against each other. I rolled my hips against him, letting out a weak groan, and he ground his erection up into me. A sordid thrill racked my body, and I fought to suppress the peak of my pleasure. This wasn't allowed to end yet.

"Please fuck me," I found myself whimpering.

Dorian stilled, but he kept his body next to mine, his quivering erection pressed against my dick.

"Are you sure?" he said.

I nodded fervently. "I need it," I found myself begging. "Please. I need you inside me."

"If that's what you want…" His words were a breath on my lips. "I will pound your fucking brains out, Rhett."

"There are lube and condoms in that cabinet," I said.

I jerked my head toward the left, knowing that if I made to grope open the small door next to the futon in this frenzied state, I would fall away from Dorian. I never wanted us to stop touching.

Perhaps the adrenaline was an aphrodisiac. Or maybe it was Dorian's body, his firm and tender touch digging into my skin, the way he rolled his hips against me. Or it was the nostalgia, the familiar scent of his skin reminding me of my frenzied youth and our forbidden trysts in the woods.

It didn't matter why. Because now Dorian was grabbing my lube and some extra-large condoms. I'd never had cause to use them before, but Dorian changed that. I knew intuitively that this reunion with Dorian would change everything.

Dorian tilted his hips away from my groin and kissed me. It didn't take him long to roll the condom down his erection, nor to lube himself up, and then his cockhead was pressing at my hole. I had thought he might warm me up first, but instead, he drove his hips forward.

I had expected my ass to clench, and I had been reflexively waiting for a stab of pain at the moment that big cock penetrated me. But the moment Dorian's latex-sheathed cockhead nudged my asshole, my ass softened, and he sunk into me like a hot knife into butter. If my ass was crying out in pain, I wasn't aware of the sting. It was like he was made to be inside me.

I cried out, too loudly. Dorian pushed forward, impaling me on his huge cock, and I saw stars. In a dreamlike frenzy, I rocked against him. He rolled in and out of me slowly, almost delicately, at first. He massaged the tense muscles in my ass with his vein-ridged cock and rendered me delirious with euphoria. I bucked my hips down furiously against him, my cock bouncing against my own abdomen with every thrust. He sped up to meet my pace.

Now, Dorian was jackhammering me, and I went limp in his arms, too consumed by sensation to move. I collapsed on top of him while he penetrated me over and over again, getting rougher with every thrust. I was suspended from reality now. Nothing existed except Dorian's body.

There was no way for me to tell how long we spent together. It was like a dream, where time didn't matter. Dorian plowed into me, over and over again. I transcended to heights of arousal I'd never even imagined before. I moaned and writhed in his arms, trying to fuck him back half as hard as he was fucking me.

"Yes!" I cried out.

I had no idea why I hadn't cum already. Every powerful punch of Dorian's cock seemed to take me a step beyond intensity that should have already torn out my orgasm. I was unable to do anything anymore except take the onslaught of his giant dick.

Dorian broke our kiss and looked me in the eyes. His pupils were vast black. His body trembled. I knew from the flush to his cheeks that he was about to lose himself to ecstasy.

"Cum for me, Rhett," he breathed.

I was compelled to obey. Throughout the haze, a rush of pleasure overtook me. Dorian trembled and seized underneath me, and my whole body tensed and relaxed at once. I fell into a bottomless abyss of arousal. This was a more powerful orgasm than I'd known was possible.

My dick shot ropes of thick, creamy cum all over Dorian's abdomen, and he throbbed his release into my ass. He was groaning, and I might have been screaming, but I didn't care if anyone heard. All I cared about was how good it felt to have Dorian's cock tearing me apart and putting me back together again.

I'd had one hell of a day, but this was the only part of it that mattered.

CHAPTER FOUR

I woke up alone in my van. I didn't remember anything from after I had sex with Dorian last night, but I must have transformed my futon into a bed before I went to sleep. I was wrapped up cozy in my comforter.

The only signs that Dorian had ever been here were the ache in my ass and the perfume of leather, cedar, and cardamon that hovered in the air and clung to the futon. I tried to inhale his distinctive musk, but with every breath I took, the smell got weaker, like the memory of a dream. I was starting to wonder if last night had happened at all, or if it had been some adrenaline-fuelled fantasy.

Yesterday had lasted an eternity. First I'd bought the pyxis—the find of my career—then I'd been attacked for it, and then... Dorian. *The one that got away had come back to me.*

Usually, I woke up exhausted and had to drink at least one and a half cups of coffee before feeling close to human again. Today, I was wired the second

I sat up, like every nerve in my body was buzzing.

I jumped out of bed and made my way to the small kitchen. Here, I had a microwave, a sink hooked up to my rainwater tank, and a small stove-top. I filled up my kettle and put it on the hotplate to boil. I might not have needed coffee to wake up, but it was an essential part of my morning.

I caught my reflection in the microwave door, and at first, I didn't give it a second thought aside from to notice I was looking pretty good today.

But I shouldn't have looked good. I should have had harsh red slashes across my face.

I ran to the mirror. My beard was in desperate need of a trim, but aside from that, I looked better than ever. My skin was clear, devoid of any scratches. I leaned forward and squinted at the mirror, dragging my hands over my cheeks. The cuts were gone, and not even thin white lines of healed scars remained. There was no sign I'd ever been touched by Mara.

The closer I looked at my own face, the more it weirded me out. Even the pockmarks where teen acne had ravaged my face were gone. My eyes were bright, devoid of the purple circles that usually sagged under them. The fine lines across my brow were fainter than usual. I lifted my shirt to examine my belly-button, where I had a small scar from my appendectomy years ago. Or rather, where I was supposed to have a scar. Now, there was no sign that I had ever had surgery.

Rather than be excited by my transformation, I

was seized by anxiety. This wasn't natural. Dorian must have done something to me last night. The only explanation I could think of was that he'd drugged me to make me forget everything after I came. But what the hell kind of drug gave you flawless skin?

I ran to my safe, and with trembling hands, I scanned my fingerprint. I knew instinctively, before the door swung open, that the safe would be empty. Seeing its barren, bubble-wrapped walls still came as an infuriating shock.

"Fuck you, Dorian!" I shouted to the empty room.

To be fair, I had already fucked Dorian, and it had been damn good. But he'd clearly been using me, exhausting me and waiting for me to fall asleep so that he could steal the pyxis. Any spark that had reignited between us last night was thoroughly snuffed out.

I had let myself think with my dick, and now I was paying for it. Dorian had changed since I knew him, turned into something dark and dangerous, but there was one thing that hadn't changed: his habit of wordlessly abandoning me. This time, instead of breaking my heart, he'd stolen my property.

I slammed the safe door closed, my blood burning. I didn't care about Dorian's cryptic warnings, his not-so-subtle threats. He wasn't going to get away with running away and screwing me over a second time.

The kettle started screaming on the stovetop. I took it off the heat with shaking hands and sent a splash of boiling water onto the ground, narrowly missing my bare feet.

A surreal haze squeezed my brain while I made coffee. To say I was confused would have been the understatement of the century. I was utterly disoriented. I should have been more focussed on the physical transformation I'd gone through last night, but if I tried to think too hard about what had happened, my temples throbbed with the promise of a migraine. It was too overwhelming. I found it easier to fixate on how Dorian had betrayed me.

And how he had fucked me.

Even furious with Dorian, I got hard at the memory of his dick. I realized I was absently fondling myself through my loose briefs, and I jerked my hand away. I wouldn't masturbate to Dorian. He would never know my private fantasies, but I would, and I refused to sacrifice my dignity like that.

Dorian already fooled me twice. I carried the burden of that shame, but I wouldn't make the same mistake a third time. I would never let him hurt me again, and I sure as hell wouldn't let him vanish for another ten years. I would find him, and I would get my damn pyxis back. I threw on some clothes, clambered into my front seat without so much as showering, and drove off.

I knew Dorian must have left town, but I had no idea where he could have gone. I racked my brains to consider any clues he might have let slip last night, but he'd been cagey about where he lived.

I idled the van outside the campsite and opened

Grindr on my phone. I was banking on Dorian being active on the apps. His sexual appetite last night made me sure he was always on the prowl. Most men didn't show their faces on Grindr, but I wouldn't need to see Dorian's face to recognize him.

I scrolled through page after page of shirtless pics until I spotted a familiar set of abs. Hardly anyone showed their face on here, but there was no way to mistake Dorian's body. I checked I was using the app on incognito so that he wouldn't see I'd viewed his profile, and I clicked into it. The little green dot under his name told me he was thirty miles away.

There were two townships about thirty miles away from my campground. One was a tiny rural town, and the other was large enough to border on being a city. If I was going to find Dorian, the latter was my best bet.

I uninstalled Grindr from my phone to suspend my account. If Dorian spotted me online, he might have been more careful. I needed his guard down if I was going to get the upper hand.

***

I stopped for breakfast at a dingy diner. Seafoam-green paint peeled off the outside walls, but it was bright inside. 80s synth-pop blasted from the creaky speakers screwed into the walls.

The coffee here was so bitter it made my taste buds curdle. I added a sachet of salt to take the edge off the burnt flavor. It made the thick, black liquid— I struggled to call it coffee—mildly more tolerable.

No coffee compared to lousy diner coffee, but no breakfast compared to good diner pancakes. Once I started eating, I was ravenous. The sweet, fluffy dough melted on my tongue like fresh cream. I devoured half the stack in five minutes.

Appetite now sated, my mind marched toward its new favorite fixation: Dorian. When we hooked up last night, he had given me no indication that it would be more than a one-night stand. I'd known that the whole time that it meant nothing, but some part of me still foolishly hoped for a real reunion. Now that hope was where it belonged. In the fucking garbage, along with my dignity.

Dorian and I were totally different men. Even when things were good between us, we had an oil-and-vinegar style relationship. He was an extrovert, and I hated crowds. He followed sports, and I spent my spare time poring over nonfiction tomes. But now, we were so different that I half-doubted he was even human. The thought would have seemed crazy to me yesterday morning, but it was no crazier than anything else that had happened over the last twenty-four hours.

I was mopping up the last dregs of maple syrup with my pancakes when I spotted a striking figure standing next to the counter in a knee-length leather dress. My blood instantly ran cold. *Mara.* Dorian unnerved me, but she terrified me. Whatever Dorian had done after I ran away yesterday, it hadn't kept her off my tail for long.

There was no reason Mara should have been after

me now that I didn't have the pyxis, but that didn't make me feel any safer. Her shoulders were drawn back, and her beautiful, too-sharp features were set into a mocking sneer.

I sunk as deep into my seat as possible, hoping I could slump so low I vanished under the table altogether. I would have run away, but I didn't want to draw any attention to myself. Now that Dorian had run off with the jar, he wasn't around to protect me from another attack.

The grey beast that had attacked me yesterday was lurking next to a shiny convertible out in the parking lot. It must have been Mara's dog. What did she do, train it to hunt down valuable relics? Did ancient artifacts have that distinct of a scent?

When I was a kid aspiring to become a real-life Indiana Jones, I dreamed of finding a magical artifact that would change my life. I'd given up on that in adulthood. I still wondered if there were things out there beyond the explanation of modern science, but if there were, I doubted I would come across them in a thrift store or market.

Everything that happened since I'd found the pyxis had me second-guessing my common sense. Mara had come out of nowhere yesterday, and the moment I saw her, I knew I was being stalked by a fierce predator. She sent chills down my spine that made me want to scream and hide. I'd been intimidated plenty in my lifetime, but Mara made me feel incomparably afraid.

She was focused on the counter for now, but she

would inevitably spot me if I stayed where I was.

I left a tip on the table and escaped to the parking lot as quickly and nonchalantly as possible, turning my head away so that my face wasn't in Mara's eye-line. I made sure not to shoot the slightest glance toward the convertible. I focused on my own van. My heart lurched and pounded harder with every step. I half-expected Mara's dog to chase me, or for her to show up behind me and scratch my face open again. *Or worse.*

I hoisted myself into my van, locked the doors around me, and looked outside. Mara's dog was staring at me, and its hungry expression made me feel nauseous. I rammed my foot to the pedal and sped away.

If Mara was chasing the pyxis, there was no reason for her to come after me again. A smarter man than me might have seen her reappearance as a reason to turn around, to give up the half-cocked mission he'd set out on. But, driven by determination—and my dick—I was compelled to continue seeking Dorian.

Dorian had been so normal in high school. When I first fell for him, he was like any other closeted jock: a veneer of arrogance covering up deep vulnerability. Once we were outed, he'd become a fierce champion of social justice and LGBTQIA+ rights. And then he vanished without a trace. I tried my hardest to find out where he'd gone, but I ran into dead end after dead end until I gave up.

Dorian wasn't the only one who'd developed new

skills in the time we'd been apart. I was going to get my pyxis back—and I would find out what had happened to him while I was at it.

CHAPTER FIVE

I got to the township of Alexander with hours to kill. It was smaller than I expected, and the streets were quiet. I hoped to find Dorian at a gay club, where horny and outgoing men tended to congregate, but they wouldn't open until night had fallen. Perhaps Alexander would be busier then.

I paid for a night's stay at a campground in the middle of town and got trapped in a forty-five-minute conversation with the woman who managed the site. I always knew when women were flirting with me, but I had no idea how to react. It was hard enough to respond when men were flirting with me—and I was attracted to men. I just nodded and stammered and laughed at her jokes until there was finally enough of a break in conversation for me to escape.

Now that I was parked somewhere relatively safe, no creepy supermodel-types in sight, I took advantage of the camp's facilities to have a shower. I scrubbed my body clean, letting a lather of soap cascade over my chest. I rubbed my loofah over my legs until all the thick hairs there were covered in creamy foam. It felt good to be clean again.

My hands drifted toward my groin. After the events of the last twenty-four hours, I knew that the second I touched myself, I would end up with an erection. It didn't matter that this was a public washroom, and only a thin curtain separated me from the other men using this room. Every time I thought about Dorian, my dick stirred.

I cupped my balls with a soap-slick hand and rolled them in my palm. I could pretend that I was cleaning my junk, but I knew that truthfully, I was desperate to pleasure myself. I fondled my balls with one hand and slicked water up and down my shaft with the other. A groan of relief escaped my lips.

You're in public, Rhett, I reprimanded myself.

I made an agreement with myself. As long as I stayed quiet, I wouldn't force myself to withstand my arousal. It was a good deal. I would keep my mouth shut, and I could let myself jerk off.

I wrapped my hand around the root of my cock and dragged it slowly up my shaft. Images of Dorian flooded my mind despite my attempts to keep the memory of his body at bay. I couldn't forget the way he had pounded me last night. He might have been using me, but anyone could get addicted to being used by that man.

Overwhelmed by the memory, I leaned against the tiled wall. If I kept my eyes open, all I saw was the flimsy, mold-speckled curtain that separated me from the rest of the room. So I let fantasy consume me and withstood the urge to cry out.

I imagined Dorian. I imagined him whipping open the shower curtain and catching me, cock-in-hand. Joining me in the haze of hot steam. I beat off more vigorously, trying to make sure I didn't pant too loudly.

"Hello, baby," Dorian said in my fantasy. He stepped closer to me, and I could have sworn I felt his body heat.

Then his lips were on mine. I stopped caring about the pyxis, about Mara and her dog, about everything except Dorian. I bucked my hips forward, as though I could rub my erection against his. It would have been easy to let go and cum already, but I drew out the anticipation, indulging in my daydream.

In my mind's eye, Dorian dropped to his knees and closed his mouth around my dick. His tongue slid around the tip of my cock and coasted down my shaft.

I needed Dorian to suck me. I needed to cum down his throat. I needed a release, and I needed him to give it to me.

Now the wet slap of my hand around my cock was distinctive enough to give away what I was doing in the shower, even though I held back my groans. I didn't care. Dream-Dorian was an expert with his mouth, almost as good as the real thing. His tongue quivered on the underside of my cockhead.

I desperately rubbed my thumb over that spot. I envisioned him licking me, worshipping eagerly at the altar of my cock.

Everything about Dorian was erotic, his gaze like lust come to life. I wanted to give him everything—and years ago, I had. Now, all I had for him were my dreams.

I slipped a wet, slightly soapy finger along my asscrack until I found my hole. I was still stretched out enough from last night that it was easy to slip a digit inside.

I rocked my hips. My cock slid through my fist, and I pushed more of my finger into my ass. I curled it to find my prostate. My finger was nothing compared to Dorian's cock, but my imagination was so vivid I managed to feel him there. I felt his lips, his hands, and his cock all at once.

I felt him pumping into me, harder and harder, driving his dick into my hole with unbelievable power. The harder I fucked myself—*the harder Dorian fucked me*—the closer I came to an orgasm.

Even though I was alone in the shower, Dorian brought me to a violent orgasm. Creamy ropes of cum spat from the tip of my cock and onto the shower floor. It was impossible to stop cumming once I started. My climax grabbed me by the balls and wouldn't let go. My legs shook, and I had to strain my thighs to keep from falling to the ground. I bit my lip, so I didn't cry out.

What was this effect that Dorian had on me? It felt like my cock spasmed and shuddered forever before I finally came down from my orgasm, and I was still overcome with aftershocks of euphoria.

My mind spun. Warm water washed away the drips of cum still clinging to my now-sensitive, softening cock. My breath was harsh, and my face was flushed from the effort of that jerk-off session.

This wasn't just about the pyxis anymore. I needed Dorian just as much as I needed my property back. I needed to taste him again, to feel his body more one time. But more importantly, I needed to make him want me as much as I wanted him -- so I could be the one who left this time.

CHAPTER SIX

fter I reinstalled Grindr, I found Dorian's profile again quickly. Now, his location was showing up as one mile away from me.

I was ashamed of how relieved I was. The first time I'd seen Dorian in ten years, he'd robbed me. Sure, before that, he had given me the best sex of my life, but that was no excuse for my sudden, obsessive infatuation. Last night had ruined me for other men—and I needed Dorian to ruin me again and again.

If Dorian was on the prowl, he would be at the biggest gay bar in town: The Ballroom. The name made me snort. *Real classy.*

Dressed in my tightest pants and a mesh top that was sure to catch attention, with diamonds flashing in both my ears, I looked like a twink on a mission —which I was. I usually hated when people stared at me, but tonight I was determined to get Dorian's attention, no matter how uncomfortable it made me.

The bouncer at The Ballroom scanned me up and

down appraisingly. He let me in without checking my ID. I wasn't sure if I should be offended. I either looked hot enough that he didn't care how old I was, or I looked too mature for my age. I hoped it was the former.

The club hit me with a wall of dance music. I recognized the song as a catchy bop from the early 2000s, and an unbidden grin stretched over my face. Now that I was in the club, the crowd was less oppressive than I expected. Everyone was caught up in their own private party: women ground against each other on the dancefloor, drag queens laughed over beers, and men made out in the queue to gender neutral bathrooms. A handful of people stared at me, but I was far from the only guy wearing fishnet.

It had been a while since I'd gone out to have fun. Technically, this wasn't a break—I was here to recover my pyxis from Dorian.

I ordered myself a cosmopolitan and sat at the bar, drinking and scanning the crowd in hope of finding my tall, dark, and handsome ex-boyfriend. There was more alcohol in my cosmo than I'd anticipated. Vodka burned my throat and went straight to my head.

I was starting to think I'd judged Dorian wrong, and he wasn't at *The Ballroom* after all, when I spotted him coming out of the restroom, his hair slightly tousled. I recognized his strut before I saw his face. He moved fluidly, like every step was a dance. I knew he must have been hooking up in the men's room, and it burned me with jealousy.

Dorian met my eyes. I abandoned my cosmo at the bar and crossed the room toward him. Everything else fell away.

A tall, lanky blonde tried to grind up against Dorian on the dancefloor, but Dorian stayed statue-still. He stared at me. The other man moved on to more eager prospects.

It felt like forever before I was standing in front of Dorian, although it must have been seconds. The moment we were within arm's reach of each other, he grabbed me by the back of my neck. The light hairs at the base of my skull snagged in his grip. I whined, but I let him pull me so close his lips rested by my ear.

"What are you doing here, Rhett?" he asked. His breath was warm against my throat, and it made my cock pulse instantly semi-alert.

"I'm looking for you," I said. "You have something of mine."

"I don't know what you mean." Dorian ground his hips against me, and his boner brushed my hip.

He was trying to distract me. *Not a chance.* The last time Dorian distracted me, he'd robbed me. No matter how much he made my balls ache, he wouldn't claim control again. He'd thrown away my trust twice already, and there would be no third betrayal. Still, he enthralled me. It would be so easy to give in.

I had no idea what sort of risky shit Dorian had gotten himself into, but I was sure it wasn't safe or natural. I knew better than to get messed up in it. I was going to get my shit and go, and if I was lucky, I might get a hookup out of it.

"You stole the pyxis. I want it back."

"Did I?" His words hummed against my earlobe, sending delicious tremors down my body.

"Yes," I managed to stammer. "You did. So give it back."

"I'm afraid I can't do that, Rhett."

I used what little resolve I had left to pull out of his grip. "Why not? What did you do with it?"

"If it's reimbursement you want-"

"It's not, and you know it. I want my property. An explanation would be nice, too."

Dorian grabbed my ass and tugged me close again. My composure was seeping away like water from a leaky bucket.

"There's an alley outside," he murmured. "Or we could use the bathrooms…"

I willed myself to keep my eyes on the prize, and I forced myself to remember that the pyxis, not this man, was the prize in question. Still, I indulged in grinding my hips against him, and Dorian let out a choked, little whimper.

Dorian wasn't the only one able to weaponize his sex appeal to get what he wanted. I pushed my erection against his. Music throbbed and swelled around us. The rest of the sweaty dance floor fell away. Dorian and I rutted together, our breaths coming in hungry gasps against each other's lips.

He kissed me before I kissed him. *My first win.* His

lips grasped for mine, hungry and desperate. I was driven mad with the urge to plunge my tongue into his mouth and devour him the way I wanted him to consume me. Every instinct screamed to give myself to this man completely, but I held onto a thin thread of common sense and teased him.

I had no idea why this was working. I was gawky, not unattractive naked, but easy to overlook in a club like this, even trussed up in pink fishnet. There were plenty of better options for Dorian to choose from. Hell, I was sure he'd been screwing around with some of them before I got here. But for whatever reason, he wanted me now. And I planned to use that to my full advantage.

I trailed my lips under his sharp jaw and dragged them over his adam's apple. I skimmed my tongue over his throat and alternated between licking his skin softly and sucking and biting him hard. I tried to stay grounded, even though every touch from Dorian, every shift of his body next to mine, made me feel like I was going to lose all self-control any moment.

By sheer force of will, I held on. I grazed my teeth over Dorian's collarbones, and his breath trembled. He squeezed tighter handfuls of my ass. He was holding me impossibly tightly now. Anywhere else, we might have gotten in trouble for public indecency, but no-one at The Ballroom cared.

"Come outside with me," Dorian crooned in my ear.

He was trying to seduce me, but I was in full control of my faculties. Whatever power Dorian had used over me last night wouldn't work a second time. Tonight, I was the one seducing him.

I slipped my hands under his leather vest and traced his abs through his tight white V-neck. This man was gorgeous beyond belief.

I chanced a glance around the rest of the room, and it was clear more men than me were captivated by Dorian. By extension, they were watching me. I wasn't built for the spotlight. I preferred to slide into the background and observe, but there was no chance of being ignored next to Dorian. If I wanted to be with this man, I would have to put on a show.

I shook off my discomfort and focused on Dorian until nothing mattered except his body next to mine. I caught his lower lip between my teeth and nipped it gently. A broken moan shivered from his lips through my bones. Dorian slipped his hands between our bodies, and then his palm was on my swollen cock, stroking it harder. The pressure was divine. I caught his eyes, and it took everything I had not to fall apart under his gaze.

Dorian played with the outline of my cock through my too-snug pants. My dick pulsed uncomfortably against my zipper. I pushed my hips harder into his grip and saw a smug smirk cross his face. He thought he was winning, but he didn't have a chance. I would be the one who emerged from this tryst victorious.

"Come outside with me," I murmured into Dorian's ear.

"I thought you'd never ask."

"I'm not asking." I flashed him my cockiest smirk.

"This is an interesting side of you, Rhett. I like it."

He followed so close behind me that his boner nudged my ass with every step. I needed that dick inside me, needed Dorian to pump me straight to heaven again. But tonight, I wouldn't let him use my hole. If he wanted me, he would have to take my cock—he would have to take everything I wanted to give him.

It wasn't cold outside the club, but it wasn't warm either. A chilly breeze skimmed over my skin, which was still flushed from dancing and hot with lust. I could see Dorian's face more clearly out here, away from the strobe lights. He narrowed his eyes and touched my face with surprisingly gentle fingertips.

"What happened to your scars?" he asked.

"I guess I'm a quick healer."

I didn't believe for a moment that Dorian wasn't behind my mysteriously fast recovery, but I was too horny to care about whatever game he was trying to play. I slammed his back against a concrete wall. I caught his wrists, pinned them over his head, and thrust my hips against him even more fervently than I had in the club. I was desperate for more, but I wouldn't take it until Dorian was begging. I needed him as distracted as possible.

"You're eager," he said.

"Speak for yourself," I growled. "You're just as hard as I am."

"Evidently." Dorian rocked into me and grinned.

He was so cocky. It took everything I had not to give in to his charms, but somehow I maintained my willpower. I released Dorian's wrists and yanked down his pants, revealing his cock. My breath hissed out. My imagination hadn't come close to recalling the detail of that perfect dick.

I was desperate to touch it. I needed to drop to my knees and suck Dorian's dick like a dutiful servant at the knees of a king.

I wouldn't give in.

I unzipped my own pants and released my own cock, already throbbing and leaking sticky precum.

"You want me inside you, don't you, Rhett?" said Dorian. He tossed his hair, more handsome and more smug than anyone had the right to be.

My ass was aching for him, but I refused to let Dorian manipulate me with his body again. I would sooner have walked away, proved him wrong, and left both of us aching and horny.

I stepped close to him again, close enough to taste his minty breath on my lips. My erection pressed against his. I wrapped my fist around both of our dicks. The silky-steel sensation of Dorian's cock against mine drew me to the gates of heaven.

"I need to be inside you," purred Dorian.

Every fiber of my body screamed at me to do what he said, but I withstood the urge. Instead, I grabbed Dorian by the hips and turned him around before he had time to react. I swept his hair away from the nape of his neck and brushed my lips there.

His skin was so hot it nearly seared me. I brushed my erection against his bare ass.

"What are you doing?" he gasped.

I yanked Dorian's pants down further so that they were around his knees. "Who says you get to be on top?"

He moaned. Dorian had groaned in bed with me before but never had his voice been so raw with depraved desperation.

I ran my fingers over his ass. Like the rest of Dorian, the skin on his ass was golden-tanned, and his asscheeks were sprinkled with a dusting of coarse body hair. Dorian was everything that turned me on in one shockingly attractive package.

I spat onto my fingers and rubbed them up and down Dorian's crack. His skin twitched where I touched it.

"I don't usually do this," he grunted.

I lightly swirled my fingertip over his entrance, and he shuddered and let out another moan.

"Won't you make an exception for me, Dorian?"

"I guess I do owe you." He pushed his hips back slightly, nudging the very tip of my finger inside him.

"Yeah, you do."

I'd spent ten years getting Dorian out of my head, and now he'd taken up residence in my mind again. If he had to occupy my fantasies, I wanted to recall as many real-life experiences as possible.

Dorian's hole was a bonus, but the price he would really be paying was higher than that. I freed my phone from my pocket and plunged my finger deeper into him, down to the first knuckle. He cried out. While he was distracted, I dropped my cellphone into the loose pocket of his leather vest.

Success.

I slipped my now-empty hand out of Dorian's pocket and groped down his abs, toward his cock. He was moaning loud enough that anyone who walked past would overhear us, but I didn't care. Anyone who veered near the alley out back of a gay club knew what they might come across. I shoved my finger forward again, and Dorian howled.

"Easy, Dorian," I murmured against his neck. I gently nipped his sweet skin. "You can take it."

"It's been a long time since I've bottomed," he said.

"But you want to bottom for me." I said it as a statement, not a question.

"Yes," he breathed.

The tight tunnel of muscle inside him softened, taking my finger completely. I felt around for his prostate, and I curled my finger to brush the sensitive spot. He let out another depraved whine. His tightly coiled muscles spasmed, the first hint of a challenge to his self-control.

Oh, this was going to be fun.

I took a brief intermission to retrieve a sachet of lube from my wallet. I tore it open with my teeth, poured it onto my hand, and slipped two fingers into Dorian this time.

Dorian gasped, moaned, and pushed his perfect

ass back against my hand.

I chanced a glance over my shoulder. The alley was deserted, nothing moving except us and the dripping rain gutter. Anxiety seized me, filling my mind with thoughts of Mara finding us and taking advantage of the distracted state we were in, but I wasn't edgy enough to stop.

I stretched my fingers out inside Dorian, and he gasped, shoving his hips back against me. He was eager for my dick, and my dick was even more eager for him. But before I gave it to him, I had to make sure he was warmed up. I slipped a third digit into him, and his cock flexed in my hand, precum leaking from the tip.

I teased Dorian like that until he was begging for me.

"Fuck me," he gasped. "Please, fuck me!"

I was on top at last. And now I was going to give Dorian what we both so desperately wanted.

I slipped on a condom and lubed up my diamond-hard cock. I rubbed my erection up and down Dorian's crack until the head was pressed against his hole. I used both of my hands to steady him by the hips, and I pushed forward. His fists were braced against the alley wall, and the four rings on his left hand glittered in the dim light.

It had clearly been a long time since Dorian had been taken like this. His ass was impossibly tight, even though I'd just stretched him out. The moment after I breached his resistance, I had to pause to let him adjust to the feeling of me inside him.

Dorian was panting like he'd just run a marathon, and the moans seeping through his parted lips were so fierce I could hardly tell whether they were pain or pleasure. But the way he was writhing, pushing his hips back against me, made it clear that he loved this.

So did I. It felt natural to be with Dorian again. Like our bodies were made for each other. I drilled him hard, cramming years of passion and frustration into every thrust. I fucked him as though one hook-up in a dingy alley could make up for ten years of abandonment.

My balls slapped against Dorian's ass, filling the alley with more sounds of sex. He groaned, and I clamped my hand over his mouth so that we didn't garner too much attention from passers-by on the main drag. Luckily, the music pouring out of *The Ballroom* was loud enough that it smothered most of the sounds we were making. I wasn't exactly quiet either. With every thrust into Dorian's tight, hot ass, rough grunts tore from my lips.

I glanced over my shoulder to check we were still in private. We weren't, but we weren't in trouble either. Our audience was wide-eyed and bearded, fondling himself through his jeans. His eyes were glued to Dorian, of course.

Our voyeur encouraged to piston my hips harder. By putting my phone in Dorian's pocket, I had already achieved my goal tonight, and I had different ambitions now. I was gonna cum. I was gonna fill his ass the way he'd filled mine. I had the power now.

Dorian pushed back against me, and we were fucking in earnest, moving in perfect synchrony. My dick flexed inside him, massaging his tightest muscles. Despite our audience, this was intimate enough to enthrall me.

Dorian released a growl that sent me spiraling over the edge. My balls tightened with the promise of pleasure, and then a brilliant release trembled through me. I slammed Dorian hard against the wall, pinned him there, and came. His ass clenched around my cock, and I knew he was cumming too. The muscles in his back rippled and shook, and I just kept on cumming, so powerfully I thought I might die from the pleasure.

My orgasm ebbed, but I stayed inside Dorian, quivering and sensitive. His ass kept clamping and softening around my cock with aftershocks. Even though the sex was over, I never wanted to pull out.

Eventually, though, my wobbling knees gave way. I stepped back and tugged up my pants. The twink who was watching us had vanished. Maybe he'd gotten his rocks off too.

Sex with Dorian was unlike any other sex I'd ever had. Being with him now was different from how it had been when we were younger. There was some intangible change in him. I liked it, even though an instinct in the back of my mind kept preaching that Dorian had become dangerous.

He turned around, leaned against the dingy concrete wall, and grinned at me. His smile made my tired cock lurch again. That smirk was pure seduction.

"Thanks for that," he said. "Would you like to go back inside and dance now?"

"How about we go back to your place for round two?" I purred.

"Am I supposed to believe you're suggesting that without an ulterior motive?"

"I don't know what you're talking about."

"Really?" He raised a skeptical eyebrow.

"Oh, you mean because you stole my property, and I want it back?"

My plan to retrieve the pyxis didn't involve Dorian extending any invitation for a more private tryst, but his dismissal still hurt. When we fucked, I felt impossibly close to him, but when it was over, it was clear his heart held no space for me.

"I'm sorry. I had to."

"You're sorry for what? Stealing from me, or-" I shook my head and scoffed. "Forget it."

"I'm sorry for a lot of things."

His apology tugged at my heartstrings, but I shut down my emotions before they could take hold. This was just another mind game, and he wasn't allowed to get in my head again. "Don't say you're sorry. Even if I believed you, it wouldn't matter."

"Fair enough." He hung his head. "My offer to reimburse you still stands."

I rolled my eyes. "Thanks for the sex, but no way."

There was no reason to keep denying myself Dorian's cash offer. I always needed money. But this was a matter of pride.

I headed back to my van and left Dorian at the club with my phone in his pocket. I prayed my plan would work. It had to.

CHAPTER SEVEN

I stared at the 'Find my Phone' application on my laptop. The little red dot on screen hadn't budged, and I was anxious that Dorian had discovered my phone in his pocket and handed it over to the bar staff.

It was just after two o'clock in the morning when the dot on-screen started moving.

My heart pounded. *This was it.* My phone traveled so fast across town that Dorian must have been in a car. Every time it paused at an intersection, my heart stammered, thinking I might finally have my target. But then the dot started moving again.

After about ten minutes, it finally stopped for good. A quick google of the address informed me my phone was at a flea motel. Clearly, Dorian didn't live in Alexander. He was passing through, same as me.

I chewed on my lip, trying to work out my next move. Dorian had been in my camper last night, so he would definitely recognize the kaleidoscopic patterns on my van if he saw me parked near the motel. If I wanted to get close to him, I would have to book my own room.

I dressed in my plainest clothes and took a cab to my destination, leaving most of my stuff behind. The less I had with me, the less evidence I could drop. All I kept in my bag was an emergency burner phone and my laptop.

It was one of those pay-by-the-hour places. A sheet of glass separated the receptionist from the waiting room. There were no chairs on my side of the glass, not even cheap plastic ones. Clearly, no-one stayed in this room for long. I spotted only three keys missing on the wall behind her: rooms 1, 3, and 5.

A woman with spiky pink hair and eyeliner sharp enough to draw blood sat with her feet up on the counter behind the glass. She tapped her long-nailed fingers against her phone and didn't seem to notice when I walked in. I had to clear my throat to get her attention.

"Hey," she said. Her voice was nasal and emotion-less. "How long do you want?"

"I- Uh-" I scrambled through my brain, trying to remember my plan. I'd thought I was ready to do this, but my mind was suddenly blank. "Two hours, to start with?"

She nodded and gestured for me to pay. I slid some cash under the glass divider. I didn't have much money to spend, considering the losses I'd already suffered over the last couple of days—*thanks, Dorian.* I would recoup it all when I got my hands on the pyxis again. I knew my obsession with the artifact was getting out of hand, but I'd committed now. I wasn't about to give up.

The woman behind the counter flipped through the cash, not saying anything. This room was so quiet that the ticking clock over her head sounded like an ominous countdown.

"Do you know if there's a guy named Dorian staying here?" I asked, breaking the silence.

The woman snorted. "People don't give me their names here. If you're looking for someone, keep me out of it."

I nodded, understanding. Places like these got by on plausible deniability.

"Is room 4 available?"

The woman glanced at the wall behind her. The key to room 4 hung between empty spaces where the keys for 3 and 5 used to be. She looked back at me. The curl of her upper lip told me that she knew exactly why I was so interested in room 4—I must have seemed like some deluded stalker—but she took the key anyway. She slipped it across the counter to me, nonetheless.

"4 is my lucky number," I lied.

"Sure. Whatever."

My room smelled like cleaning products and mothballs. The stench of ammonia assaulted my senses. At least it had been sterilized recently, I figured, as I took a tentative seat on the double bed. It creaked dramatically under my weight. The floral-patterned comforter was so old I half-feared it would crumble when I touched it. But for all its dilapidation, the bed held me up comfortably enough.

I turned on my computer and logged into the motel's WiFi to check that my phone was still nearby. According to the little red dot on the screen, it was only a few feet away.

A duet of debauched moans was coming from room 3, but neither voice belonged to Dorian. The man sounded guttural and hoarse, like he smoked three packs of cigarettes a day, and his partner's voice was high and shrill—not Dorian's type.

I put my ear against the torn wallpaper on the other side of the room to eavesdrop on room 5. Low murmurs met my ears, but I couldn't make out who was talking or what they were saying. I retrieved up a dusty glass from the wobbly-hinged drawer in the kitchen and gingerly pressed it against the wall.

I recognized Dorian's distinctive drawl, and my heart skipped a beat. I'd gotten lucky.

"-safe for now," he was saying, "but I haven't shaken my tail. I need to find a way to get it to safety or destroy it before things take a turn."

Destroy it? I flared with rage. Dorian had no right to destroy a priceless artifact. The pyxis belonged in a museum.

There was a long stretch of silence before Dorian spoke again. He must have been on the phone. "Of course, sir. But Mara's not the only problem."

Was he talking about me?

"Yeah, that guy. He found me at a club tonight."

He was definitely talking about me. *That guy.* Was that all I was to him? His apathy shouldn't have stung, but it punched me in the gut.

"He's smarter than I expected."

Wow. *Rude.*

Another pause, and then Dorian said, "I suppose I could slip into his dreams, but he's already suspicious. Do you think it's worth the risk?"

What did he mean, *slip into my dreams*? An uneasiness settled into my bones. I should have left. Packed up and cut my losses, fled from this nightmare. But I kept my ear against the glass, and the glass pressed up against the wall.

"I'll get rid of him."

I never believed Dorian's apology in the first place, but now it rang malicious. Tears threatened to sting my eyes, but I set my jaw and blinked them away. I'd cried over this man too much already.

"I'm concerned about that too," said Dorian.

Concerned about what?

The bed in Dorian's room creaked. "Is there any way you can take it?"

I had expected Dorian to pawn the pyxis, but I was still gripped by anxiety at the thought of it changing hands.

"I know it's my job. But it's a complicated situation."

More silence.

"No, sir. I swear it's not like that. He doesn't mean anything to me."

Dorian's words brought a bitter taste to my mouth. I wished I'd never started eavesdropping, but now I couldn't stop. Everything Dorian said made me despise him more.

"Thank you. I really-"

Another pause.

"Okay. Tomorrow night."

Dorian must have hung up, because now there were no sounds from the room next door. I wanted to move, to sit down and recoup, but I was frightened that Dorian might hear the glass rubbing against the thin wall if I budged. I stayed frozen in place. Thoughts raced through my mind, and panic battered the insides of my skull.

I had to stay focused on the task at hand. My window of opportunity was shrinking, and any festering feelings could wait until later. I needed to get that jar back before Dorian met with his mysterious associate and I lost the trail forever. Dorian had spoken on the phone with deference, and anyone Dorian deferred to must have been terrifying.

I needed to get the pyxis back within the next two hours. I didn't relish the idea of paying for more time in this shithole motel. Once I got my hands on the jar, I could get out of Dorian's life. He could get rid of me, like he wanted. But he wouldn't get away with the pyxis.

Someone more professional than me would have taken Dorian up on his offer yesterday. They would have taken his money, handed over the pyxis, and booked it. Had it really been my moral code that made me refuse? Or had I wanted to keep Dorian around for five minutes longer? I shook my head as though I could physically toss away the thought. It was too late to think about that now. I was hooked on whatever game he had me playing. Any professionalism I might have claimed was in tatters. Now, all I cared about was winning.

No. That wasn't strictly true. I cared about making Dorian lose.

Dorian's bed creaked again, and I thought maybe he was settling to go to sleep. But only a few seconds later, it became clear I was wrong. Dorian wasn't going to go to sleep—at least, not without jerking off first. Tinny male moans made their way through the wall, and it became clear that Dorian was watching porn. Apparently, sex with me hadn't been enough to satiate his voracious appetite.

My cock was immediately rock hard yet again. I pictured it all too clearly: Dorian, on his back against one of these dingy comforters, his legs spread. I imagined him pulling down his pants, letting his cock flop out, probably already swollen hard. I fondled my own junk through my pants, listening to moans and grunts and occasional spanking sounds.

I was halfway through pulling my dick through my fly when I realized I had an opportunity to do more than get off. Dorian was distracted. *This was my chance.*

I left my room quickly and somewhat awkwardly, on account of the substantial bulge in my pants. Outside, the night air was chilly, and I wished I'd put on a thicker jacket. I marched down the road, away from the motel, until I was standing outside a strip club.

I had an emergency phone in my bag. It was a Nokia from the early 2000s, the kind of invincible mobile that could outlive a cockroach in a nuclear attack. I dialed my own phone number into the greyscale screen.

"C'mon, pick up," I muttered.

I felt out of place here. The other men outside the strip club were laughing, competitively guzzling beer, and hollering at any girls unfortunate enough to walk past the crowd. They reeked of alcohol, and they might have broken me in half if they thought I was checking them out.

"Hello?" Dorian picked up my phone, breathless. I wondered if he had cum yet, or if I had interrupted him while he was still jerking off. My cock twitched unhelpfully.

"Hey, you've got my phone!" I spoke louder than I had to and intentionally slurred my words so that Dorian thought I was drunk, rather than playing a strategic hand.

"Is this Rhett?"

"Yeah, who's this?"

"This is Dorian."

"So first you steal my pyxis, and now my phone!" I pretended to sound indignant.

"I didn't steal your phone, Rhett."

"Where are you? I'll come get it."

"There's no way you're getting my address. You're not as smart as you think you are."

It took everything I had not to snort into the phone. Dorian was underestimating me, and that made my upper hand even more satisfying.

"Then just bring my phone to me, I don't care."

A group of men cheered loudly from a couple of feet away. Their raucousness made me increasingly uncomfortable, but at least the noise would make my lie more convincing to Dorian.

"Where are you?"

"I dunno, some club." According to the neon sign over the entrance, I was outside The Blue Lounge, but I wasn't telling Dorian that.

"I can't bring you your phone if I don't know where you are, Rhett." Irritation seeped into Dorian's voice. He definitely thought I was off my face drunk. *Good.* I wanted to piss him off. This was all a game to him -- *I* was a game to him -- and I was going to win.

"I can head back to the campsite now if you bring my phone there!" I told him the address, intentionally stumbling over my words as though my tongue was tangled with liquor.

"I'll meet you there." His voice was tight, agitated. Exactly how I wanted him.

I hung up the phone, slung my hood over my head, and headed back to the motel. I stayed in the shadows and walked with my legs splayed out to the side, adopting an exaggerated swagger. I hunched my shoulders to guard my body language—

the less chance of Dorian driving by and recognizing me, the better.

CHAPTER EIGHT

I was starting to think I'd gone crazy. It would have been much simpler—and probably much safer—to get a big, fat cheque from Dorian and pretend I'd never seen the pyxis at all. But I'd come so far that giving up was no longer an option, and besides, thoughts of the pyxis consumed me. Dorian was the only thing that distracted me from that accursed clay jar. They were interconnected in my mind, both irresistible.

I got back to the motel five minutes after I called Dorian and lured him away. The locks on the doors here were old and easy to break. I jammed my credit card into the doorframe's seal and tilted the card from side to side. The locks probably hadn't been replaced since the 90s, because it took less than ten seconds before I jiggled the door handle open.

I knew instantly that I was in the right place. The scent of Dorian's sweet musk was imprinted in my memory. Even in this bleach-soaked room, the oaky notes of his cologne were unmistakable. My phone was nowhere to be seen, of course. Dorian had already taken it across town.

I rummaged through a bag of Dorian's clothes. I found an astronomical amount of lube and condoms, but no sign of the pyxis. *Had he taken it with him?*

My heart palpitated, and I worried it would seize in my chest. I was terrified of getting caught in this room, even though all I was doing was stealing my own property. I yanked open the drawers in the bedside cabinet, but I didn't find anything there either.

I was about to give up when, on a whim, I checked the bathroom. *Nothing.* I opened the cabinets under the sink just to be sure.

A rich oak box sat next to a maze of rusty pipes. I knew instantly that it was valuable, which made me confident it didn't belong to the motel. I pulled it out to get a better look. The box was only the size of my head, but it was as heavy as if it were made of pure iron rather than wood.

I gingerly put the box on the floor and sat cross-legged to examine my discovery. It was a puzzle box, at least two hundred years old, although I would have had to take it back to the van to date it precisely. Gold inlay patterned the sturdy wood with occult symbols. I had figured out already that Dorian was involved in something dark and dangerous, and this box all but confirmed my suspicions. My ex-boyfriend wasn't the man I thought he was. Maybe it was better for both of this that he pushed me away.

The pieces of this messed-up puzzle were starting to come together, but I couldn't make sense of the picture. My stomach twisted. I should have left, but curiosity compelled me to stay.

The solution to break into the box wasn't immediately obvious. I considered smashing it open, but the wood was too robust, and besides, the treasure hunter in me couldn't bring me to destroy something so precious. I could have called a cab and run away with the whole thing—once I was done with it, the box would fetch a hefty price—but I had to play this smart. And the smart thing to do was get the box open, take the pyxis, and leave everything exactly how I'd left it. Then I could vanish without a trace, and Dorian would have no way of knowing I'd been in his room until it was too late. By the time he figured out the jar was gone, I would be miles away.

If my plan went smoothly, I didn't know when I'd get to see Dorian again. *Probably never.* He'd be rid of me. I ignored the pang that shot through me. Dorian had started this. Ten years ago, when he left me with nothing but a gaping hole in my chest where my feelings for him used to burn, he had earned karmic justice. Stealing the pyxis from me had sealed his fate.

I brushed my fingertips over the puzzle box. The wood was cool from being under the sink. I felt for panels that would move under my touch and tried to let everything else fall away, going into an almost meditative state. No matter which I touched it, the box remained unresponsive. I breathed deeply so the time pressure wouldn't freak me out so much. Panic would only make this worse.

It was as though I could hear the pyxis calling for me from inside the box. My heart pounded, and I fought to keep my hands steady. I danced my fingers across to another panel.

At last, I heard something click. The box still wouldn't open, so I felt around until I heard another click. Then another. After four clicks, the box swung open.

The pyxis sat in the middle of the box, reflected from every angle by its mirrored walls. A wreath of herbs surrounded the jar. I didn't recognize any of them except for dill and sage. At the very back of the box lay a black knife with a double-edged blade. I ignored my better instincts and picked it up. Like everything else in here, the knife was old, and if I had to hazard a guess as to its use, I would say it was a ritual artifact. My stomach churned.

It wasn't that I thought Dorian had killed someone. It was just that I no longer had any idea what was possible. If he had told me he sacrificed humans in exchange for sexual potency, I wouldn't have been surprised. I had reached a state of mind where I was unshockable.

When we were together the first time, Dorian never said anything that would make me think he'd start experimenting with the occult. He had been so normal back then, focused on sports and student politics, planning to undertake a degree in psychology—science, not magic. He and I were like any other teen lovers: stealing kisses when we were alone, finding excuses to slip out of our houses in the middle of the night and rutting together whenever we thought we were alone. Dorian had been the first man I'd fallen for. He'd been the first man to break my heart, but I never thought he was physically dangerous. Clearly, I'd been wrong.

An ordinary man didn't hide out in motel rooms with stolen artifacts and bloody daggers in sealed puzzle boxes. Over the last ten years, something had changed Dorian irrevocably. I wished it would scare me off, but I didn't want to leave.

Even though I was alone, I felt like I was being watched. I glanced over my shoulders, half-expecting to see someone behind me, but there was no-one there. I breathed deeply, put the dagger back in the box, and plucked up the clay jar.

Relief swept over me once I had the pyxis in my hands once more. My fingers grew warm where I touched it, and the heat echoed through my body. I didn't notice how much I had missed it until I was holding the jar again. My shoulders relaxed, and I grinned more broadly than any intruder in a cheap motel had the right to smile.

Compulsively, I tried to open the jar. The lid was still jammed shut, but it seemed like there was more give than yesterday—or maybe that was wishful thinking.

How was it only yesterday that I had bought this little jar? Just yesterday that I'd reunited with Dorian? It felt like it had been at least a week since I'd met with the elderly shopkeeper to purchase this artifact. So much had changed in a day and a half.

I put the pyxis gently on the ground and worked out what to do next. The moment I lifted my hand away, the euphoria that had settled on me lifted. Now that my skin was no longer touching the jar, the air chilled. I needed to get out of here. I clutched it tightly between my palms again, and I was instantly soothed.

My only plan was to get back to my van and drive as far out of town as possible, away from Dorian's reach. Unlike him, I would disable Grindr before I went on the run. A twinge of loss snagged my gut, but I pushed it out of mind. He deserved this, especially after that fake-ass apology. He deserved to have something he cared about taken away.

I left the bathroom. The moment I stepped into the main room, my blood froze in my veins. There was a hulking beast of a dog standing right next to the bed. *Mara's dog.* My stomach twisted. I didn't know what was going on, but I knew something was very, very wrong.

CHAPTER NINE

I stared at the dog, and the dog stared back at me. It's sharp, pointed muzzle twisted into an expression more human than canine, like a leer or a mocking smile. The eyes, too, were starting to look uncanny. The pupils shrunk until they were ringed with red irises.

I stumbled backward, staring helplessly at the door behind the dog—my only escape, just out of reach. When I looked back at the animal, it had become even more monstrous. The back legs were too long now, the knees bent at an awkward angle, and its muzzle was shrinking into its face. I wanted to make a break for it, but I was frozen in place.

The dog—*not a dog*—rose onto its back legs. It was as tall as a human now, and its hair was starting to draw back into its skin, revealing pale skin underneath. My stomach churned so much I thought I might vomit on the motel carpet.

The creature's sick smile widened.

I was going to die.

Any reasonable person would have dropped the pyxis, but I couldn't bring myself to part with it. Ever since I first touched it in that antiques store, the jar had been mine. If I wouldn't let Dorian have it, I sure as hell wasn't going to give it to this *thing*.

At least Dorian fucked me before he stole from me. This creature was more likely to kill me to take what it wanted. I prayed Dorian would come back and save me like he had saved me from Mara, but he was on the other side of town, at the campsite. *Thanks to me.*

The beast's transformation was almost complete, and with a sick twist in my gut, I saw a naked man in front of me. He was still covered in a thin layer of still-receding tawny fur, and his mouth was full of razor-sharp teeth.

I should have sold Dorian the damn jar.

The pyxis was getting even hotter in my hand, hot enough that it should have burned my skin.

I was only eighteen when I left home. I'd been desperate to run away from my dad before his violence left marks that would last longer than bruises. Mostly, I'd focused on getting out. But deep inside, I had hoped I might discover something amazing, something that would alter my life forever.

What a stupid hope. This brush with adventure was going to kill me. Mara's dog-man was going to kill me.

I gripped the lid of the pyxis tightly, and it shifted under my fingers. I fumbled to twist it. I wasn't sure what would happen if I got the jar open, but judging by how many people were after the arti-fact, whatever happened was sure to be dramatic.

The lid was still stiff under my fingers. I twisted it further, but the dog-man reached me before I was able to get it open. Even though he looked human now, his breath reeked of raw meat. There was only a thin layer of fur on his face now, but his expression was twisted into a threat.

I thought he would wrench the pyxis away from me, but instead, he grabbed a fistful of my hair and forced me to look at him. His eyes glowed red. I looked into them and heard distant screaming. The more I faced down this monster's stare, the more I fell into it, and the more painful it was. It felt as though flames were crawling up my spine.

"Give me the jar," the dog-man whispered hoarsely, "and I might let you live."

I shook my head stupidly.

He grabbed me by the throat, and I suddenly found myself struggling to breathe. This was it. This was how I would die. I kept clinging to the pyxis, even as a scream of pain ripped through my suddenly-parched lips. Dorian had been telling the truth about at least one thing: it would have been safer if I stayed away. The dog-man's eyes bore into me until pinpricks of light dotted my vision. Then everything went black.

CHAPTER TEN

I woke up naked, in an unfamiliar bed, with a raging erection. Satin-smooth sheets swaddled me and made my bare skin tingle. The ceiling rippled and glittered above me, and the windowless walls shimmered.

"I've been waiting for you," purred a familiar voice.

I sat up and spotted Dorian in a plush leather chair on the opposite side of the room. His usual playful smirk was absent, and his brow was scrunched in concern. Rage, relief, and arousal fought for power over my pounding heart.

A silk dressing gown was cinched around Dorian's waist, the top half tumbling open to expose an expanse of smooth muscle. His nipple piercings glinted in the light. My cock twinged, the way it always did around him. No matter how much he pissed me off.

Focus.

"Mara's dog- It stole the pyxis-" As soon as I

opened my mouth, I was yelling, unable to hide my terror. "What the hell is going on?"

Dorian's jaw twitched. "Mara has the pyxis?"

"What's going on?" I asked. My voice cracked up an octave. "Where's that… That thing? And where am I?"

"You're with me. You're safe. Now, did Mara-"

"Bullshit, I'm safe with you." The words were out before I could stop them.

"You don't have to trust me, but you need to tell me what's going on." His voice was low, urgent.

"I don't *need* to tell you shit."

Frustration flashed over Dorian's face. "Like it or not, I'm the only one who can help you now, Rhett."

He walked toward my bed with the grace of a ballet dancer, seemingly in slow motion. Despite my terror, I was transfixed by his body. It was impossible to be around Dorian without wanting him. But there were more important things to think about than sex.

I folded my arms. I might have looked more intimidating if I wasn't butt naked. "I'm not answering any of your questions until you answer mine."

"Always so curious." Dorian smiled tightly.

"How do I know you're not behind this? I know I don't mean anything to you, so why are you even here?" I spat out the words. If Dorian wanted to get rid of me, he'd have to stab me in the front this time.

"What are you talking about?"

"I heard you talking on the phone in the motel."

Dorian took a seat on the bed, next to my knees.

The mattress dipped under his weight. "You're quite the detective, aren't you? I suppose you planted your phone on me at the club so you could track me down. Smart."

If he was trying to flatter me, it wouldn't work. "Just let me out of here."

"I can't let you out."

"Sure, you can't." I rolled my eyes.

"I literally can't." He spread his fingers and held up his palms, supplicant. "I don't have that kind of power."

"What kind of power?"

"You must have figured out by now that things aren't what they seem."

"A dog just turned into a man in front of me. Yeah, I'm well-aware things are fucked."

Dorian snorted.

So tell me what's real. And try not to manipulate me this time."

"I'm sorry you overheard that phone call."

"Yeah. Whatever." It was better I knew the truth.

"I have enemies. They can't know about any attachments."

I wished I could trust him. The earnestness on his face made him seem all too easy to believe. But to believe him, I had to believe he was attached to me. That was plainly untrue.

"Do you always refer to your enemies as 'sir'?"

"You overheard me talking to my boss. My job doesn't allow for relationships. If I told him that I'd fallen for someone-"

"Please." I rolled my eyes, even though my heart skipped a beat. "Don't do this. We both know you just want the pyxis."

"I do want the pyxis. But I want you too, Rhett. I've missed you."

"Fuck you, and fuck these mind games."

"I need you to trust me." Frustration edged into Dorian's voice. "If you don't, you could get hurt."

"And if I do trust you, I won't get hurt?" I scoffed.

"Rhett…" Dorian pinched the bridge of his nose. "We don't have time for this. I'm sorry. I'm sorry for everything. You have to believe me."

"You've apologized before. I didn't believe you then, either."

"How can I make you trust me?"

"Tell me the whole damn truth for once." I threw up my hands, exasperated. "Who is Mara? What was that thing that came after me? And why the hell does everyone want that jar so much?" I had other questions too -- questions like *'why did you leave me?'* but I didn't want to sound pathetic.

"What do you think?"

"I have no idea." The only answer that sprung to mind was too ridiculous to put into words. "If I knew, I wouldn't be asking you, would I?"

"Come on, Rhett. Don't sell yourself short. You know your classical history. What do you think might be so important about an unopenable ancient Greek vessel?"

"I- I, uh-" My voice broke. "I can't think of anything that doesn't sound stupid."

"After all you've seen today, how can anything sound stupid?"

"Is it Pandora's Box?" I mumbled.

I was right. That did sound stupid.

A proud smirk crossed Dorian's handsome face. "I told you you knew."

"You're fucking with me."

"I'm not."

I should have been laughing in Dorian's face, demanding the real truth. But the last twenty-four hours had been so impossible any answer would have sounded surreal. That I had happened upon Pandora's Box was as likely as any other explanation.

"What does Mara want with Pandora's Box?" I asked.

He sighed. "Do you have to interrogate me now? This situation is time sensitive, and-"

"Yes. If you didn't want to be interrogated, you should have told me the truth upfront. What does Mara want with a box of sins?"

"Mara is a demon," said Dorian simply.

A hot sweat broke over my brow. The smooth timber walls seemed as if they were closing in, shrinking the strange room around me. I hated how much Dorian's answer made sense.

"I see," I said, eerily calm considering how much I wanted to scream. "And that thing that attacked me?"

"He's her hellhound."

"Her hell... hound?"

"Yes. Hellhounds are sent up from the underworld to retrieve items for their masters."

Items like Pandora's Box.

"What kind of demon is Mara?" Were we talking about some kind of trickster or a princess of Hell?

Dorian's amber gaze suddenly burned red, striking me with a flashback to the hellhound's feral eyes. I would have collapsed to the floor if I wasn't already lying down.

"What the hell?" I yelped.

I scrambled back on the bed, away from him. My dick twitched.

"She's the same kind of demon as I am," Dorian said.

"And w-what kind of demon are you?" I stammered.

"I'm an incubus. And that's the truth."

Dorian was a sex demon. Of course no-one else compared. My shoulders dropped in relief. That explained the boner.

"And Mara is a succubus," Dorian continued. "That means we-"

Suddenly, I understood why the walls were swimming, why the bed seemed so big, and why I felt like I was melting into it.

"I'm dreaming, aren't I?" I said. It was so obvious, now that I knew. "Incubi come to you in your dreams."

"Yes. This is your dream, and that's why there's nothing I can do to pull you out of it. What we have to do-"

"If this is a dream, where am I, really?"

Dorian sighed. "There's no way for me to know where Mara and her hellhound took your body. I can only meet you in your dreams."

"Why didn't she just kill me?"

"She can't kill you. The pyxis has chosen you as its new guardian. As long as you're touching it, you can't be harmed." Dorian put his palm on my knee. His hand was gentle, comforting. *Erotic.* I struggled to think about anything except how much I loved his touch.

"So what? I'm the new Pandora?" I managed to see.

"More or less."

"What happened to the old Pandora?"

His face hardened. "There are some questions you don't want to know the answers to."

I wanted to know the answer to everything, but I knew better than to push it right now. He was telling me what I needed to know. I could ask more later, if we survived this.

"Why are a succubus and an incubus fighting over Pandora's Box?" I asked.

Lines of frustration creased Dorian's forehead. "Mara wants to open Pandora's Box in the underworld. If the jar is opened on earth, there's a chance to shut it before too much damage is done, but if its contents get released in hell, the effects on the human world will be catastrophic. Over half your population will become dangerously violent in a matter of hours, and it'll only get worse from there.

It'll make The Purge look like a children's movie. I'm talking about the total destruction of humanity, if not the annihilation of humankind itself. "

"Oh, is that all?" I said weakly.

"So, to stop that, we need to-"

"Why do *you* want Pandora's Box?" I interrupted again. "Why am I supposed to believe you aren't trying to steal it off me so you can get the credit for destroying the world instead of Mara?"

"There's nothing I can say to make you believe me," said Dorian. "All I can do is hope you will."

"You're a demon. Why should I trust you? Isn't evil your thing?"

"No. *Sin* is my thing. There's nothing inherently evil about lust, is there?"

"I-"

Dorian sidled closer to me. I choked on my own breath. The look in his eyes was as wicked as hell itself, but I saw no menace there. He leaned in, and I thought he was going to kiss me.

Instead, he whispered in my ear, "I've told you the truth. Do you trust me now?"

"Not completely."

But I wanted him. It might have been the adrenaline, the relief of having a fraction of my questions answered, or maybe it was Dorian's demonic pull. No matter the reason, I needed to be with him. I grabbed him by the back of his head, knotted my fingers in his hair, and pulled him into a kiss. His lips were hot and passionate, as eager as my own. I slipped a hand under his silky robe. Every atom in my body vibrated with anticipation when my fingers met his hot skin. I lay back, and he loomed over me. His kisses landed on my throat, butterfly-light

"Are you sure you want this?" he murmured.

I nodded.

"Good." His voice was lower now, almost a growl.

He mouthed further down my neck and sucked marks onto my skin. I fell into the feeling. It was so powerful it nearly made me pass out again. *Could you faint in a dream?* His teeth nicked my skin, and I wouldn't have cared if he drew blood.

My blankets had vanished into thin air. Now, I was naked, exposed to him. He wrenched his lips away from my throat, knelt between my legs, and looked at my body as though he was starving and I was a four-course meal.

I'd be anything he wanted as long as he didn't want me to back down.

Dorian leaned forward again. His lips found my collarbones, and he dragged his tongue toward my clavicle. His kisses danced over my pecs and toward my trembling abdomen. The way he touched me was pure indulgence. His dressing gown tumbled off his shoulders, uncovering strong back muscles rippling under golden skin. All of my blood pumped away from my brain, and I was dizzy with desire.

It wasn't enough. I tugged off his robe and pulled him down so he was lying, naked, on top of me.

The skin of his erect shaft met my cockhead, and the friction made my eyes roll back into my head. Pleasure had overcome all sense of reason. Despite everything, nothing had ever felt more natural than fucking my incubus ex-boyfriend in my own dream.

He slowly made his way toward my aching cock and nuzzled my groin, breathing deeply. His breath made my erection throb more intensely. He swirled his tongue around the base, and nothing else mattered anymore.

Almost nothing.

Before I got too carried away, I forced myself to sit upright. "If Mara wants to destroy the world, why are we fucking around right now? Why aren't we trying to stop her?"

"We are trying to stop her," said Dorian. He stopped rocking against me, but his heavy body still pressed down on mine. "How much do you know about incubi?"

"Not a lot. I've studied history, not mythology."

Dorian looked at me with the kind of raw vulnerability I hadn't seen since we were teenagers. "I can keep you safe as long as we stay in your dream, but Mara is trying to wake you up. You can't stay asleep forever, and I don't want to think about what might happen if you wake up alone. If I want to fight Mara, I need strength."

"And to get strength, you need to feed on me?"

Dorian nodded.

"And feeding is… Fucking?"

He nodded again. His weight shifted, making me shudder and gasp.

"Won't that make me weaker, though?"

"No. As long as you consent, it's a mutually beneficial relationship."

"I definitely consent."

As soon as I gave my permission, he was kissing me again. His tongue dominated my mouth, and I was at his mercy.

"What, exactly, is the plan?" I gasped when we broke apart.

"Feeding is easy, but all the strength in the world will be useless if I'm nowhere near Mara and your physical body. If you wake up while we're making love, I might be able to follow you."

"That's one hell of a pickup line," I managed to joke. I wished Dorian wouldn't say *making love.* The love boat had sailed across the horizon long ago.

"What do you say?" asked Dorian. "Will you let me fuck you again?"

I nodded. "Please. I need you."

Dorian crawled between my legs and positioned his mouth over my cock. I braced myself for the onslaught of pleasure.

"Try not to wake up until I say so," he said. Doubt soured his expression, but only for a moment. "We have one chance to save the world."

Dorian licked from the root to the tip of my erection. He swirled his tongue over my cockhead. The sensation stole my breath with its intensity.

I squeezed my eyes shut. When I opened them, I was alone in a cold room, and my dick throbbed, untouched. The pyxis seared the skin of my palm. *Not yet.* I closed my eyes again and let exhaustion wrench me back into my dream, as though I was fighting my alarm clock early on a cold morning.

"You have to hold off," I heard Dorian murmur. "Please."

I fisted my hands in the silky sheets. This might have been a dream, but it felt real beyond reason. My skin was alight with ecstasy.

Dorian's hot, wet tongue flickered over that sensitive spot where my shaft met my cockhead, and my body writhed responsively. Dorian moaned. I tangled my hands in his hair, pushed his head down, and plunged my cock deeper into his throat. He only gagged for a moment before he began bobbing up and down more urgently, taking me to unparalleled heights of pleasure.

I slipped into consciousness again.

"No," I whimpered aloud. "Not yet-"

"Dorian's got him!" a rough voice growled.

Mara's voice was unmistakable. "That's not poss-"

I slipped back into slumber.

Dorian surfaced. "Don't let them wake you up," he said.

"You've got to fuck me," I said. "Mara knows you're here. We don't have much time."

Dorian swore under his breath and sat upright. I parted my thighs and bared my hole to his erection.

"Fill me up," I begged. "Fuck me!"

There was no time for any more foreplay. Dorian gripped my ankles, steadied them at his shoulders, and lined up his cock with my entrance. He pressed forward. The good thing about dreams, I supposed, was that there was no need for lube. He thrust all the way inside me in one fluid motion. My body shuddered with pain only for an instant before all-consuming pleasure took me over. I cried out, exalted, and bucked my hips responsively.

Dorian's perfect dick filled me up like it was made for my ass. He took me more roughly with every thrust. He fucked me with an urgency I'd never felt before. I clutched him tight. Even in my dream, the scent of his sweat was intoxicating.

I slipped my tongue into his mouth and scraped my fingernails down his back, making him moan against my lips. His depraved cry made me throb from the inside out. His abs against my cockhead took me to another dizzying height of pleasure.

"Harder," I gasped.

Dorian slid almost all the way out of my hole and shoved deep in again. He massaged the tight passage of muscle inside me over and over with his demanding shaft. I let myself fall into the sensation, let it fill me up. It was more evident than ever that Dorian wasn't entirely human. No normal man could fuck me this well.

My balls tightened, and my breath quickened. *Not yet,* I pleaded with my body.

Dorian slipped away from me again. Reality found me in a room like a jail cell, surrounded by nothing but damp concrete walls. I thrust my hips upward, but my cock touched nothing except empty air. I missed Dorian's solid body.

Mara's frantic voice met my ears, but before I

made out what she was saying, I was back in my dream-room with Dorian's dick inside me. Nothing else mattered.

"Fuck-" I cried. "Fuck, I'm gonna cum-"

No sooner were the words out of my mouth than Dorian's body stiffened over me. With a grunt and a powerful thrust, he slammed my ass full of thick, creamy cum. His passion heated up my bones. Warmth flooded my body. I was cumming too. My cock spasmed and released a powerful blast of jizz between us.

The force of my orgasm woke me up properly, only this time, when I came to consciousness, Dorian was still on top of me. My pants were around my knees, and my fingers were fixed like concrete around Pandora's Box.

CHAPTER ELEVEN

Neither Dorian nor I had time to react before Mara's dog-man dove at us. Even in his human form, a short layer of bristly hair covered every inch of the hellhound's naked skin. The hellhound wrenched Dorian away from me, tugging his dick from my aching hole. I jerked up my pants one-handed so that I wasn't left exposed.

"Kill the incubus," Mara's cool voice ordered. I spotted her standing in the corner of the room, half concealed by shadow. She smiled, as cruel and beautiful as ever. "Leave the human. For now."

"No- Dorian!" I yelled.

The hellhound punched Dorian squarely in the jaw.

"Hold onto the pyxis, Rhett," said Dorian. He rubbed his handsome jaw where it was red from impact. His voice was calm, despite everything.

"Whatever happens, don't let go."

Even if I wanted to let go, it would have been impossible. The pyxis was sealing itself to my palm with enough heat to burn me, but my skin stayed unmarred. The explicit etchings in its clay walls glowed blood-red, and it trembled as though someone had turned on a vibrate function. I touched the lid, and to my shock, it shifted under my thumb. It was like the pyxis wanted me to open it.

Dorian took a swing at the hellhound. It became clear that no matter how rough he was in bed, he only used a tiny fraction of his real strength with me.

One punch to the gut sent the hellhound slamming back so violently that the concrete wall cracked where he landed against it. In a flash, Dorian was in front of him, and his hand was around the demon's throat. They were both naked, both inhuman monsters, but even in this fight-to-the-death, every movement Dorian made was graceful and erotic.

The hellhound snarled, revealing canine teeth. I shuddered. That half-human, half-beast leer was just as unsettling as when I first saw it.

Dorian leaned in so close to the hellhound that I thought he was going to kiss him. But instead, he inhaled deeply. The hellhound let out a weak moan. His hairy cock sprang erect, and revulsion churned my stomach. Dorian released the hellhound's throat, and the demon sunk to the ground, apparently incapacitated.

Mara took advantage of Dorian being distracted.

She swiped at him, and he howled in pain, a sound I'd never heard from him before and never wanted to hear again. Long red scratches sliced open his back, and blood instantly pooled at his wounds. She had cut him deep.

"Dorian-"

Dorian spun around to face Mara, his fist raised, but before he struck her, she gouged at his chest. He screamed again and fell onto all fours. Rivulets of scarlet were spilling over his strong back, and his newly cut-open chest dripped blood onto the hard concrete floor. I hadn't expected Mara to be stronger than Dorian, but apparently, I had underestimated her.

My fingers burned and ached around the pyxis. Even though I was no expert on classical mythology, I knew that the last time this box was opened, it hadn't gone well for anyone. I didn't want to unleash all the sins of the world. But opening Pandora's Box was sure to cause one hell of a distraction. It would give Dorian a fighting chance again.

Mara kicked Dorian's ribs over and over with the pointed toe of her black leather boots, and he fell flat on the floor, smeared red with his own blood. The hellhound had transformed back into his canine form now. He advanced on Dorian with knife-like teeth. I couldn't stand to witness him be tortured like this. I refused to watch him die. If there was any chance I could help him, I had to take it.

I made eye contact with Dorian. His jaw was clenched, lips twisted in silent pain. His eyes blazed the same shade as the etchings on the pyxis. There could be no denying what he was. He glanced from my face to the jar in my hands, and he nodded, so shortly and sharply that if I had blinked, I would have missed it. But I didn't blink. I wrapped my hand around the rim of the pyxis's lid, and I pulled it open.

A white mist spilled from the jar and poured through the room, filling it with blinding white light. The fog felt like acid on my skin. Through the haze, the only thing I held onto was the sight of Dorian's hellfire-filled eyes. My heart stammered, and before I knew what I was doing, I was stumbling toward him. As long as I kept looking at Dorian, the smoke around me couldn't harm me, no matter how much it hurt.

Mara was screaming, and her hellhound was howling. The pyxis was as hot as if I was cupping lava in my palms. The longer I held the jar open, the louder their screams became.

I fell into Dorian's arms. He touched me, and the pain faded. Dorian hugged me tightly. His lips found their way to the sensitive spot beneath my earlobe, and he whispered urgently in my ear, "You need to close it. *Now*."

The lid resisted my attempt to jam it back down. It was like trying to force two repelling magnets together. I pushed harder, encouraged by Dorian's lips on my neck.

"You can do it," he murmured.

His faith in me made me want to believe in myself. My muscles strained as though they would rip in half from the effort it took to push the lid down.

The white mist around us slowly squeezed back into the pyxis. It was like watching a mushroom cloud in reverse. If I let go before Pandora's Box was sealed shut, I knew it would spring open again. I wasn't sure I had the strength to shut it twice. The pain was incomparable.

I was glad that Dorian was holding me up. Without him there, I wouldn't have had the physical or mental strength to go on. I would have let those blistering plumes of smoke spill out over the whole continent. My arms shook, and tears streamed down my face. He kept kissing my neck, murmuring encouragement in my ears.

With one final push, I tore the last of my resolve from my spent body and forced the lid shut.

The pyxis went cold in my hand. The etchings on the side were lifeless. It looked like any other museum artifact—ancient and precious, but otherwise ordinary.

I spun around, looking for Mara and the hellhound. The room was empty except for Dorian and me. A cold chill shuddered down my arms, and I lost control of all my muscles. I slumped limp. Dorian gently lowered me to the ground.

"What's going on?" I managed to murmur.

"You have no idea what you just did, do you?"

I shook my head. "Where's Mara? And the hellhound?"

Dorian plucked the pyxis from my grip.

"Mara and her hellhound are in here," he said. A genuine smile played on his lips and lit up his face. He tapped the side of the jar.

"How- Why- What?" My head spun.

"I can explain everything later. You need to rest."

Dorian kissed me gently on the lips and scooped me up. The cut that stretched from his collarbone over his pecs throbbed blood onto me.

"Are you okay?" I asked.

"I'll be fine," he murmured. "I've got you."

And I had him. How could an honest-to-god demon make me feel so safe?

CHAPTER TWELVE

I woke up cozy and warm, sure I was swaddled in my familiar bed and reeling from a vivid nightmare. Then I opened my eyes. Maybe I was still dreaming.

I was in a vast, brightly lit room, all pale wood, red brick, and windows so vast the walls might as well have been made of glass. A snow-capped mountain range loomed in the distance, dotted with green trees that looked like children's toys from this far away.

That view was nothing compared to the beautiful man silhouetted in the window. Sunlight streamed past Dorian's broad shoulders and narrow waist, making him look even more striking than usual. A genuine smile wiped away his trademark cocky smirk.

"Good afternoon," said Dorian.

"It's the afternoon already?" I asked dimly.

"Yes. You've slept for fourteen hours."

I didn't actually care what time it was. All I cared about was the breathtaking, heartstopping man in front of me. Satin slacks clung to Dorian's impressive bulge, and a thin white shirt hung open to bare his chest. Angry, red marks from Mara's attack were slashed across his skin. Yesterday came back to me with a flash of adrenaline.

Dorian must have seen the fear cross my face, because he said, "Don't worry, Rhett. You're safe now."

I wanted to believe Dorian, but my blood was still racing. I sat up, and midnight-blue bed sheets fell to my waist. Last I remembered, I had been wearing a T-shirt smeared with Dorian's blood. Now, I was shirtless, clean, and wearing silky pants that matched his own. He must have changed my clothes while I slept. I yawned and wiped sleep from my eyes.

"You know you could have woken me up earlier," I said.

"I wanted to let you rest. You deserved it after yesterday." Dorian's voice was so sweet and earnest that a blush rose to my cheeks.

"It wasn't that big of a deal," I mumbled.

"You survived opening Pandora's Box." Dorian sat on the bed next to me. It sunk slightly under his weight. "And then you managed to close it again. Most humans would die trying. A lot of demons, too."

"I- That can't be true." There was nothing special

about me.

"It is true." Dorian sat next to me on the bed. I thought I might crumble under his gaze. Even if I had been fully dressed, I would have felt nude under his probing stare. He cupped my chin and tilted my face up so I had to look at him. "Just trust me when I say you saved the world."

"Me? *How?*"

Dorian smoothed my hair away from my forehead and pressed a kiss there. I thought he might tease me about my relentless questioning. Instead, he gave me one of his first straight answers.

"Honestly, I don't know," he said. "You're an enigma."

I laughed. Dorian was the complicated one, not me. I opened my mouth to ask him another question, but before I got a word out, he shut me up with a kiss. Rational thought fled my mind. Dorian's touch was just as satisfying as the information I sought so desperately. I slipped my hands between us to feel the ridges of his abs. My fingertips met the rough scabs where Mara had slashed him, and I pulled away.

"Are you okay? Mara hurt you pretty badly."

"I'll be okay after I have sex again," said Dorian. He must have noticed the shock that crossed my face, because he chortled. "I'm an incubus, remember? That's how it works."

I understood that. What I didn't understand was why Dorian hadn't healed himself already. "Why didn't you just go to a bar and hook up with someone else?"

"Because I didn't want to hook up with anyone else." A flicker of concern crossed Dorian's face, and he pulled away from me.

"Is that a bad thing?"

"No. But it's not normal, and if my superiors found out…"

"Your superiors?" My mind was beginning to spin. I knew more than ever before, and I felt like I knew nothing. "What superiors?"

Dorian pursed his lips. "I can't-"

"Don't say you can't tell me. That's bullshit." I crossed my arms defiantly. "If you don't tell me, I'll find out myself."

Dorian's lips stayed pinched together, but amusement sparked in his eyes. "Alright, Rhett. I'm forbidden from telling you everything, but I'll answer what I can. What do you want to know?"

I had so many questions, they all tripped over my tongue. I looked around the room, seeking inspiration as to what I should ask first. My eyes landed on a cramped bookshelf.

"Where's the pyxis now?" I asked.

"Pandora's Box has returned to its rightful home."

"Which is…?"

"In a museum."

"Can I see it?"

"Humans aren't allowed in this particular museum."

A shiver ran down my spine. "Then how can I

know the pyxis is safe?"

"Because the world isn't on fire." As if sensing that his answer wouldn't satisfy me, Dorian offered an apologetic shrug and smile. "Even if I wanted to take you to the museum, I wouldn't be allowed. There are rules."

"Rules set by your superiors?"

"Yes," said Dorian. He touched my thigh, and electricity soared through my body. "Hell is more than fire, brimstone, and screaming souls, Rhett. Different demons have different jobs that come with different privileges. My job is to hunt down certain powerful artifacts and make sure they don't end up in the wrong hands."

"Like Mara's hands?" I recalled her talon-like fingernails and repressed a shudder.

Dorian nodded. His hand crept higher up my thigh, making my cock twitch. I forced myself to stay focused.

"When I woke up alone in that cell, I heard Mara yell that it wasn't possible for you to be there," I said. "Why?"

"Ah." Dorian pulled away from me, sighed, and massaged his temples. "Of course she mentioned that."

"You asked what I wanted to know," I pointed out.

"I should have presumed that the answer would be 'everything'." Dorian sighed. Not only had he stopped touching me, he wouldn't meet my eyes. "Mara put protective wards around your cell to keep me out. I got past them."

His answer was flippant, and it didn't match his severe expression.

"What do you mean, protective wards?"

"Back when people believed in demons, they came up with magic to keep themselves safe from us. They compressed that magic into powerful sigils, which we call wards. Usually, wards are hidden in old buildings, carved into stone and sealed off where no one can see them, but demons don't know the old sigils. We have our own. Mara's were drawn in chalk on the door to your cell, and they were only designed to keep me away."

I waited for him to give me more information, but he offered nothing.

"How did you get past her wards, if they were designed for you?" I pressed.

Dorian's forehead creased into a frown. "You probably won't believe me, but I have no idea. She's stopped me before. The only thing different, this time, was you."

"What about me?"

"I wish I knew."

"Take a guess."

Dorian swallowed and wet his lips. Time stretched out for what seemed like forever before he spoke again. "My working theory is that your soul was somehow corrupted by us being together when we were young and innocent. Now, we have a bond that's stronger than anything Mara anticipated."

I felt light-headed. I knew that my first love left a mark on my heart. I had no idea it had *corrupted my fucking soul* as well.

"So you were an incubus back then, too."

I didn't know why I had assumed Dorian had been human the last time I knew him. Maybe because he seemed so normal in high school. Maybe because I didn't want to accept that everything we had was a seduction.

"Yes and no. Technically, I'm a cambion."

I racked my brains to work out why that word sounded so familiar but came up with nothing. "What's a cambion?"

"Cambion are the offspring of demons and humans," Dorian explained. "You remember how my mom raised me alone, right?"

"I remember." I remembered everything about Dorian. "So that means your dad is an incubus?"

"Yes. I met him a week before I left town, and he told me everything. Before then, I had no idea what I was. I didn't even know I had powers."

"But you *did* have powers?"

"I swear I didn't use them on you. I loved you for real. And if you loved me back, that was real too."

"I loved you," I said, quicker than I needed to. "I've never loved anyone like I loved you."

He combed his fingers through my hair, his expression so tender it stole the breath from my lungs. "You deserve a life free from demons. I thought that leaving would protect you, but it must have been too late. Now, we have this bond. I don't know how to keep you safe."

I didn't know what to say to Dorian when he was this raw and emotional, starkly different from the man I'd been playing cat-and-mouse with over the last two days. I chose to return to the familiar: asking questions.

"Do you think that our bond, or whatever, is why the pyxis chose me to be its new guardian?"

Dorian smiled slightly. "Probably. Pandora's Box is a jar of sin."

"And you're basically a sin dealer."

Dorian snorted. "That's one way to put it."

He moved as if to kiss me again. I stopped him before our lips met. I needed more answers, and if I let him distract me with his body, I would never get them.

"Is Mara a cambion too?" I asked.

Dorian rolled his eyes. "No. Mara is a full-blooded succubus. She's stronger than me, but she relies on her strength to get what she wants. You're lucky you're gay. Our charms only work on people who are attracted to us."

"I guess that is lucky," I said.

"Now, do you have any other questions, or can I finally kiss you?"

"Just one more question for now," I said.

"Ask away."

I looked Dorian right in his stunning amber eyes, and a flush heated my face.

"Am I dreaming again?" I asked.

"No. You're not dreaming."

"Then kiss me."

I leaned back into the bed, pulling Dorian on top of me. His chest was warm against my skin, and when our lips met, I felt the smile in his kisses. Nothing existed anymore except Dorian, me, and this beautiful moment.

The urgency that had compelled us to fuck so brutally over the past two days had ebbed. I thought I had lost Dorian forever years ago. Somehow, he'd returned to me, and he wasn't going anywhere again. We were inexplicably, irrevocably bonded together.

Dorian's lips left my mouth to brush my throat, and the nerves there tingled straight to my cock.

Since our reunion, Dorian had been the only feature of my fantasies. The idea of being with another man hadn't even crossed my mind. I assumed it was Dorian's charm and our history that fixated me to him. Now, I wondered if it was something more profound.

It didn't matter why I wanted Dorian. All that mattered was that I had him. I rocked my hips up, and he ground his weight down upon me. His erection flexed through the satin between us. The thin barrier was too much. We needed to be naked.

I tugged Dorian's pants off, and his cock slipped out. It poked against my stomach, leaking with pre-cum and leaving a warm streak where it touched my skin. I released a depraved moan.

Dorian rolled over, and before I knew what was going on, he had pulled me on top of him. His cock was swollen rock-hard between us. I rolled my hips down, pressing the weight of my still-covered shaft against his naked erection.

"Tease," gasped Dorian.

Dorian gently pushed my shoulders, encouraging me to crawl down the bed. I knew what he was asking for, and I was more than happy to give it to him.

I kissed my way down Dorian's chest, tugging gently on the silver bars in his nipples and making him gasp, then skimming my tongue over the lines of his abs until I reached the swathe of dark, trimmed pubic hair by his crotch. I inhaled deeply, enjoying the perfume of this perfect man.

I lavished his balls with light strokes of my tongue and swept them into my mouth. The high whimpers that escaped Dorian's lips were intoxicating, and they encouraged me to suck harder. He groaned appreciatively.

I kept sucking Dorian's balls until Dorian started jerking himself off. I knocked his hand away.

"That's my job," I said.

I wrapped my fist around the base of Dorian's cock to hold it steady, and I pressed my tongue to the tip. I savored the flavor of his sweet precum. He moaned.

"You are very, very good at your job," he said.

I shivered at the compliment. Dorian had probably slept with more people than I'd ever met, and he was still choosing me. Encouraged, I stretched my jaw and let the bulbous head of his cock slip past my tongue and into my throat. I made sure to keep my mouth sloppy with saliva. I loved sucking Dorian's cock. I could have done it forever. I let him slot deep into the back of my throat, and he moaned. Encouraged, I increased the pressure around his shaft by sucking my cheeks in.

Dorian fucked my face harder, and one of his hands came down to grip the back of my head and hold me in place. I moaned around his cock, and he swore under his breath. His grip on me tightened. I rolled his spit-wet balls in my palm and sucked his cockhead.

My own cock was throbbing, and I found myself rocking down into the bed, practically humping the covers in my eagerness. Hot adrenaline still lingered in my blood.

Dorian gently tugged my head up, freeing his dick from my mouth. A strand of saliva still clung to my lips and the tip of his cock. The red slashes on his chest had faded to hard white ridges of scarring. I met his eyes.

"I want you to fuck me again," he said.

How could I say no to that?

I licked my way down the map of veins that curled around Dorian's shaft to skim my tongue over his balls. He tilted his hips up, giving me better access to his ass. I gripped handfuls of his solid glutes, spread his cheeks, and dragged my tongue to the rim of his hole. He moaned.

Encouraged, I swirled my tongue and pressed it down, driving into his entrance. I held onto Dorian's thighs and explored as deep as possible before my jaw ached. Every taste and smell of this man was perfect. Dorian was sex incarnate.

"God, Rhett- I need you inside me- Please-"

I sat up and hooked Dorian's legs over my shoulders, angling him so that my erection was poised by his hole. I spat on my dick to lube it up, even though with Dorian, lubricant seemed unnecessary. He was always ready to fuck.

I touched the tip of my pink-flushed cockhead to Dorian's hole.

"Fuck me," he demanded.

I thrust forward, watching in awe as my erection impaled Dorian. His hole stretched pink around my shaft and squeezed tight around me. Inch-by-inch, I filled him up. Dorian cried out, a sound that made my balls clench and my cock throb harder. His back arched, and I thrust forward again, now buried to the hilt in his tight hole.

I fell forward onto Dorian, still inside him, and our lips found one another. We devoured each other. I wanted to fill him up completely.

I kissed Dorian hesitantly at first. Our kisses fast became more frantic, and the lazy pumping of my hips was replaced by violent thrusts. My balls clapped against Dorian's ass, filling the room with the sound of sex. I fucked him harder, grunting and groaning with every thrust.

He kissed my chest and scraped his hands over my back and my ass. The rings around his fingers were shockingly cold and smooth in comparison to the coarse heat of his skin. His nails bit into the hollows by my hip bones, eliciting shivers of pain that only intensified the pleasure I felt. I thrust harder, falling into a quick rhythm now. My breath was starting to hitch with depraved gasps, and I knew I wasn't going to last much longer before I reached my climax. The pleasure was building up powerfully, and it would erupt soon.

Dorian must have been able to tell that I was close, because he broke our kiss to whisper in my ear, "Fill me up, Rhett. Make me yours."

Dorian had given me phenomenal orgasms before, but nothing compared to how I felt when this dam broke. The moment he gave me permission, my cock exploded with white-hot pleasure. The earth shattered around us. I thrust erratically and pumped his ass full of my cum. He moaned and writhed under me, his body quaking, and then I felt something hot and thick spilling between us, and I knew he was cumming too. His ass clamped down around my seizing cock, and I thought I might die from how good it felt.

Pleasure seemed to rip apart my body. My climax scattered my atoms into the universe and brought me back together, only to destroy me again. Another rope of cum burst from the tip of my cock and blasted into Dorian's ass. He moaned, and I cried out.

It felt like our orgasms lasted forever. Eons seemed to pass before I came down from the heady rush. I collapsed onto Dorian's chest, gasping.

Dorian caught me in a kiss, and we lay like that

for a while, my cock still twitching in his ass, his cum sticky between us. I didn't ever want to move, but eventually, I rolled off him. I immediately missed the pressure of his ass around my well-used cock. His chest was covered in creamy jizz and devoid of any scars. He was a vision of perfection, better than any fantasy.

"You're not wounded anymore."

"You fucked the pain right out of me." Dorian's laugh was jarringly carefree.

I traced my fingers over where his injuries had been hot and red less than an hour ago. "Is sex with you what made my scars vanish too?"

"More questions already? At least let me get my breath back."

I giggled. "Sorry."

Dorian panted next to me for a few long moments. I was about to repeat my question when he answered me at last. "Incubi and succubi heal ourselves with sex. I've never heard of that power transferring into a partner, but I can't think of any other reason your scars vanished overnight. It's... Bizarre."

"Do you think it's because of our bond?"

"Most likely." Dorian traced his fingers over my lips, making me tingle. "I guess we can't fight this, can we?"

"I don't want to fight it."

"I don't think I could fight it even if I did want to," murmured Dorian.

Dorian's words knocked the breath from my

lungs as violently as if I'd fallen from a skyscraper. I'd fallen, alright, but he caught me before I hit the ground.

I tried to stay rational and withstand the desperate pleas of my heart. "But you're- You know."

"A demon?"

"Not just that. You're rich."

I gestured wildly around Dorian's bedroom. The view must have been worth a million dollars, and Dorian's bed alone probably cost more than everything I owned put together. Ostentatious diamond cufflinks winked at me from his mahogany dresser. This kind of luxury was foreign to me.

"Ah, yes. That reminds me. I have an offer for you."

"I'm not giving up everything I've worked for to become a trophy boyfriend," I said.

I regretted the words the moment they left my mouth. Dorian hadn't asked me to be his boyfriend. Incubi weren't allowed to date.

"I'm not asking for you to stop working," said Dorian gently. "I'm offering you a career opportunity. If you take it, you'll be earning more monthly than that pyxis was worth."

"Working for you?" I wrinkled my nose. "That sounds even worse than being a kept man."

"Working *with* me. You'd be working for my boss."

"Isn't your boss the devil?"

"He's *a* devil."

A steady paycheck was tempting. I wasn't too

sure about the boss from hell.

"Doesn't your boss sorta hate me, though?" I might have understood why Dorian said the things he said, but that phone call still replayed in my head.

"He doesn't hate you. He doesn't know anything about you. I'm not allowed relationships, but there's no reason he has to find out about that. I'm allowed to fuck whoever I want, even colleagues."

My stomach flipped. "So we're in a relationship, are we?"

Dorian's rarely blushed, but his face was suddenly scarlet. "If you want to be."

"I-" I should have said no. I had taught myself to guard my heart against men in general, and it was all because of Dorian. But looking into his eyes, all I could say was, "I'd love that."

"And the job? I mean, we work similar jobs already. We might as well team up."

I raised a doubtful eyebrow. "I trade antiques. You hunt magical artifacts."

"I said we work similar jobs, not identical ones."

"Why would you want me on your team? I don't have any special powers." I hugged my arms around my waist.

"Most old buildings are warded by ancient sigils to keep demons out. Any building older than a hundred years is most likely warded. Unfortunately for us, that's where a lot of demonic artifacts end up being kept. If you've ever walked into a church, you can do something no demon can."

"Were there wards around the antiques shop where I bought the pyxis?"

Dorian nodded. "When Pandora's Box was inside the shop, there was no way for me or Mara to sense where it was. If anyone other than you had taken it outside, Mara might have gotten her hands on them, and we would be living in a very different world right now. That's exactly why you'd be such a valuable associate to me. You're book smart *and* street smart, you think on your feet, and as much as your endless questions annoy me, you're a fantastic investigator."

"And I can walk into churches."

"*And* you can walk into churches." He smirked. "You're perfect, Rhett."

"Thanks." I blushed. The compliments were too much. Dorian's offer was fast becoming more and more tempting. This could have been the big break I wanted—albeit not the one I had been expecting.

"So what do you say, Rhett? Will you work with me?"

My mind reeled. How many times had I dreamed about these kinds of adventures? *Almost as many times as I'd dreamed about being with Dorian again.* The opportunity of a lifetime had fallen into my lap. All I had to do was take it.

"Okay," I mumbled. My tongue felt too big for my mouth. "Okay, I'll do it."

"Really?" he said.

It was hard to reconcile Dorian's eager, earnest gaze with the eyes that had shown me visions of hell itself.

"Really. But if I'm taking this job, your boss already owes me for Pandora's Box." The words sounded strange to my own ears.

"I'll talk to him tonight," said Dorian.

Dorian pulled me into another soulful kiss. Every doubt and fear vanished from my mind. I had no idea what I was getting myself into, but as long as I was with Dorian, I didn't care.

ABOUT THE AUTHOR

Micah Hayden aims to blend his passion for thrilling stories with his passion for hot guys by writing about vampires, demons, and other sexy, supernatural deviants.

When he's not reading and writing, Micah can be found either relaxing at home with his long-term boyfriend or out dancing at the local LGBTQ+ bar.

CONTENT WARNINGS

Explicit M/M sex scenes; body horror; mention of homophobia and drug use